BY COLBY RODOWSKY

Spindrift

Spindrift

COLBY RODOWSKY

FARRAR STRAUS GIROUX / New York

Library of Congress Cataloging-in-Publication Data
Rodowsky, Colby F.
    Spindrift / Colby Rodowsky. — 1st ed.
        p.   cm.
    Summary: During the summer after seventh grade, Cassie sees her
close-knit family life in Bethany Beach, Delaware, changing drastically
as her older sister has a baby, reveals the true nature of her husband,
and announces the breakup of her marriage.
    ISBN 0-374-37155-5
    [1. Sisters—Fiction.   2. Divorce—Fiction.   3. Babies—Fiction.
4. Bethany Beach (Del.)—Fiction.]   I. Title.
PZ7.R6185Sp   2000
[Fic]—dc21   99-36263

To Franny and Helen

SPINDRIFT

One

MEGAN AND TOMMY AND I were up on the board-walk after supper, eating frozen yogurt to celebrate the end of school and the beginning of summer, and that we'd made it through seventh grade and particularly Mrs. Quattlemayer's English class. "Move onward and upward, ladies and gentlemen," she had said that afternoon as she collected the test papers. "Onward and upward, with nary a mixed metaphor among you."

"Onward and upward," said Megan, her tongue darting around the edges of her cone to catch the dribbles.

"I'm not even sure I'd know a mixed metaphor if I met it head-on," said Tommy.

"She accidentally let the cat out of the bag and really put her foot in her mouth," I said.

"Who?" they said at the same time.

"Not *who* but *what*," I said. "That's it. A mixed metaphor. I think."

Megan groaned and Tommy said, "Give it a rest, Cassie. School's over." And we all three slouched down on the bench, propping our feet on the railing in front of us and staring out at the ocean.

Now, to clarify a bit (Mrs. Quattlemayer is big on "clarification, ladies and gentlemen, clarification"): Megan Mallonee and Tommy Layton and I have been best friends since kindergarten, when we were the only three kids in our grade who lived right in town and not scattered around the county someplace. We've always done just about everything together and have made a blood pact to stay friends forever, do something incredibly dramatic when we grow up, and *never* leave Bethany Beach. Which is going to be hard to do because Bethany isn't all that exciting. Except, to us it is.

The thing about Bethany is that it really is the "quiet resort" it's known as. I mean, there aren't any roller coasters or boardwalk trains or glitzy hotels. Instead, there are houses, and a lot of little shops that sell T-shirts and frozen yogurt and books and film.

There are restaurants, a couple of small motels, a handful of churches, a post office, and a library. There are also shells and sand and seagulls, and the ocean waves that just keep rolling in.

And in the winter things get even more quiet. When we were younger, Megan and Tommy and I used to walk the boardwalk end to end on cold windy days, making up an elaborate story as we went, all about how we were the last people left in Bethany (and on Earth)—and how we would survive.

As for me, I'm Cassie Barnhart—tall, basically shapeless, and with sort of chopped-off straw-color hair that mostly looks windblown. Two important things to know about me are: (1) I don't eat anything that has a face; and (2) I fix things: smooshed-down sand castles on the beach, lopsided bird's nests that the birds have long since abandoned, clocks, and some-times life. At least I try.

After we'd been sitting there awhile, Tommy stood up and stretched, saying, "Let's go. There's nothing happening here and I have to start work at seven to-morrow."

"At least you have a *job*, a real one," said Megan, shoving the end of her cone into her mouth and pitch-ing the paper napkin into the trash.

"Only because my parents own a bakery," said

Tommy. "And because they got me working papers and are making me work the early shift, which means I have to get up at 6 a.m. *all summer.*"

"Okay, but they're also *paying* you," said Megan.

"Yeah, minimum wage and all the jelly doughnuts I can eat, but hey, I'm not complaining. It's *steady* minimum wage. I think my folks finally figured out that they had an untapped labor source right under their roof. Anyway, Megan, think of the money you'll be raking in baby-sitting all summer."

"Yeah, sure, it's not exactly easy money, baby-sitting for a bunch of kids who think being on vacation means never having to say they're tired," said Megan.

"Makes no difference, on account of there's good money to be made from the invasion of the touri, right?" said Tommy.

The invasion of the touri is what we call it every June when the tourists arrive from Wilmington and Philadelphia and Washington and Baltimore. When they fill up the houses that have been closed and empty all winter long, swarm into TCBY after supper for their frozen yogurt, and plant their umbrellas and sand chairs on the beach that the three of us like to think of as mostly our own.

"And speaking of the touri, I'll be working at the Spindrift again, naturally," I said.

"Same old stuff?" asked Megan.

"Same old stuff," I said. "Changing beds and doing laundry and cleaning up rooms."

The Spindrift is the bed-and-breakfast that my grandmother Emma has run since before I was born, and where Mom and I still live. Where Cindy, my sister, lived too, until she married Mickey, my favorite and only brother-in-law—and moved into his house a couple of miles out of town.

A bed-and-breakfast is a place to stay for people who don't like big hotels. What's cool about the Spindrift is the rooms look like *real* rooms and have names instead of numbers (Ebb Tide or Sandpiper), and everybody eats breakfast together, either in the dining room or out on the porch. There's a piano in the living room, and a TV, and a whole shelf of games and puzzles for rainy days. I used to close my eyes and try to count up all the people who had stayed at the Spindrift since I was little, but I gave that up a few years back. Some I remember, and some I don't.

"What did your grandmother say when you told her you want to get a waitress job as soon as you're old enough?" asked Megan, pulling me back into the conversation.

"Not much, really, because, you know, she put the Spindrift on the market last fall and hopes it will be sold soon. But, either way, she knows that eventually I can make more money in the summers by waiting tables than I can with her. Anyway, come on, let's go."

We walked across the boardwalk and down the ramp, our shoes scritching against the sand on the street as we headed home. A couple of blocks up Atlantic Avenue, we came to a yard that was swarming all over with people, some moving in and out of the house while others perched on the rail fence or huddled around the grill. There was sort of a low-key thrum of music, interrupted every once in a while by the sound of laughter, and the greasy smell of cooking burgers filled the air.

"Whoa, party time," said Tommy, pulling himself up and straddling the fence. "Let's go in."

"You crazy?" said Megan.

"We can't just go someplace where we don't even know the people," I said.

"Sure we can. Besides, we do know them. At least some of them," said Tommy, swinging his other leg over and sliding down the inside of the fence. "My brother Scott's supposed to be here. He was telling us at supper about this party being given by a girl he works with at the Adobe House. She has a huge Great Dane and long blond hair. Come on."

When Tommy saw that Megan and I had stayed put on our side of the fence, he called back to us, "Did it ever occur to you two that Scott just might have *invited* me? Invited *us*?"

"Might have—but didn't, right?" I answered him.

"Well, yeah, but that's only because he didn't think of it. Now, come on. We'll only stay long enough to get something to eat."

"What happened to getting to bed early, the morning shift, all that stuff?" asked Megan.

"That's why we'll only stay long enough to get something to eat," said Tommy, waiting as Megan and I made it over the fence.

"I'll get the sodas," he said, taking off across the yard. Meanwhile, Megan and I drifted over to the grill, attaching ourselves to the back of the crowd and trying to look older than we actually are, and hoping that no one would ask us who we were or what we were doing there. Double hoping not to encounter either the Great Dane or the girl with the long blond hair.

We grabbed three rolls. I piled mine high with tomatoes and onions and a ton of ketchup, which I actually like, while Megan stood there like some Oliver Twist look-alike, hoping someone would put burgers on hers and Tommy's.

All of a sudden Tommy pushed up behind us, taking us by our elbows and saying, "Come on, let's get out of here."

"What's wrong?" I asked, turning to look at him. "Did somebody say for us to leave?"

"No, nothing like that," he said. "It's just that there's not much doing here and I still have to get up early and—"

"Forget it, Tommy," said Megan. "You dragged us in here, and now we're starving and we're not leaving till we get something to eat. That yogurt just didn't do it."

"If you hold my sandwich and wait here with Megan," I said, "I'll go find us some Cokes myself."

I headed for the washtub by the back steps and had just fished three Cokes out of the ice and was drying them on my jeans when I looked up and saw my brother-in-law standing in the shadows. "Hey, Mickey!" I called. "Where's Cindy? I didn't know you guys were here." But my voice was swallowed up in a sudden surge of music as someone cranked up the volume.

Still holding on to the Cokes, I started over to where he was standing. "Hey, Mic—" My words froze and hung there as I watched a girl with a long red braid come up behind him and wrap her arms around his waist. He turned to face her, pulling her even closer, locking his mouth over her mouth, and running his hands up and down her back. They stood there swaying, sort of squirming against each other in a way that made me feel sick, until what seemed like hours later the girl broke away, looping Mickey's arm around her shoulder and saying, "Come on, let's go someplace private."

"Mickey, no! Don't!" I cried out, but the two of them turned without looking at me and went toward the street. And I knew, from the way my throat felt tight and dry, that the words were still locked inside me.

I let go of the Cokes and heard the cans hit the ground. I felt someone take me by the arm and turned to see Megan and Tommy standing in back of me. "*Now* will you get out of here?" Tommy said as the two of them steered me through the gate and onto the street.

"You knew, didn't you?" I said when we had gone a little way. "You knew and that's why all of a sudden you wanted to leave. Right, Tommy?"

"I saw them when I went to get the drinks, sort of wrapped around each other there in the middle of everybody's coming and going. They weren't exactly into noticing, though, and I didn't think you needed to see that."

"Was that *really* Mickey?" I said, shaking my head. "I mean, it couldn't have been, on account of Mickey would never—not in a million years—do that to Cindy. And especially not now that she's about to have a baby almost any day. He just wouldn't, is all."

"Come on, Cassie," said Megan. "Let's go to my place. We can sit on the porch and—"

"I want to go home," I said. "I just want to go home." I started to walk, my face burning and the rest of me shivery cold.

I could hear the other two coming along behind me, and when I got to the Spindrift, I turned and waved.

I took a deep breath and went inside.

Two

"THERE'S A STORM BREWING," my mother said as I walked into the kitchen, letting the screen door slap shut behind me. "And a big one, at that."

I blinked at the light and swallowed hard, half afraid that just by looking at me she could tell what I had seen. That she knew what I knew.

"A storm?" I croaked. "A regular storm?"

"Of course a regular storm. You just came in from outside. Do you mean to tell me you didn't notice the clouds, and the wind coming up? The last day of school really must've gone to your head."

"I guess," I said, picking up the pots and pans I'd left drying on the drainboard and shoving them in the cupboard. "Where's Emma?"

"Gone for a walk with Will. He has a plot twist he

wants to talk out with her, but I hope they pay attention to the weather."

Will Porter has been vacationing at the Spindrift for ages, and every year he comes oftener and stays longer, even in the off-season. If he suddenly stopped coming, though, Will is one of the guests I'd remember, no matter what. He's old but not really *old*, in the same way that my grandmother Emma is old but not really *old*. He's a mystery writer, and he brings along his laptop and sits up in his room (always the Sandpiper) and works for hours at a time. Will set one of his books in a bed-and-breakfast in Bethany Beach, Delaware, like ours, only he called the house Spinnaker instead of Spindrift and made it white instead of brown. A hardcover copy of *Murder Takes a Vacation* always sits on the front-room table, and when guests want to borrow it Emma reaches into a shopping bag and hands them a paperback copy. Sort of the way some B & Bs give out mints or chocolate-chip cookies. My personal opinion is that Will has a thing for Emma.

Any other time I would have rolled my eyes at my mother and said, in my sexiest voice, "A walk in the moonlight, huh? Just the *two* of them?" But there wasn't any moonlight, and a storm was coming. I couldn't stop to talk because all I really wanted to do

was get off someplace by myself and try to sort out the
thoughts racing through my head.

"I'm going out to look at the waves," I said, grabbing a windbreaker from the closet and hoping my mother wouldn't decide to come with me.

"Okay," she called after me. "But be careful and on your way check the porch and make sure the rocking chairs are up against the wall."

I went through the hall and out onto the porch, pulling the front door closed behind me. I stopped to move the chairs, then followed the narrow-board walkway that led to the beach. The wind caught at me and spun me around, and I braced myself against the lifeguard stand, which lay on its side, pulled out of reach of the surf.

Mickey did.
Mickey didn't.
He would.
He wouldn't.

The words beat inside my head as I stared at the ocean.

The wind picked up, and a spitting rain began. A crowd of girls came along the shore, tossing a volleyball back and forth from one to the other. I watched until they disappeared into the darkness. Then I saw this white-haired couple coming toward me, holding hands, his pants legs rolled up, her hair blowing in the wind.

All of a sudden I recognized Emma and Will and ran to meet them. By the time I got there, they weren't holding hands anymore—and were standing about three feet apart.

The two of them holding hands was definitely portentous, I thought, dragging up one of Mrs. Quattlemayer's favorite words.

As I looked from one to the other, Will said, "Weather's picking up some. Looks like a regular northeaster settling in."

"Are you coming in, Cassie?" asked Emma, shouting to be heard over the wind and nodding in the direction of the house.

"In a while," I said. "I want to stay out a little longer."

"Okay, but don't be too long, especially if there's any lightning," she said, and she and Will hurried across the beach in the direction of the Spindrift.

I stood there for a few minutes, watching the waves rise and crash against the shore. Then I pulled my hood up over my head and went back to the lifeguard stand, settling down beside it and locking my arms around my knees.

"*Mickey would never do that!*" I shouted, straining my

voice to carry over the crashing surf. "Never in a thousand years." But even as I said the words, pictures were flashing in my head. Mickey with that girl. Mickey kissing her and rubbing his hands up and down her back, pressing his body against hers.

I shook my head and dredged up other pictures, forcing them over the ones already there, thinking back to Cindy and Mickey's fairy-tale wedding three years ago.

It was absolutely the most beautiful ever. Anywhere. Anytime. It took place on the beach, right on this very spot, only with the lifeguard stand pulled over to the side. On a Tuesday morning in June, at eight o'clock, with the whole Atlantic Ocean as the backdrop, a lady minister in a long, white robe and bare feet presided. There were sand chairs arranged in rows on the beach, down close to the water, and all the guests wore shorts and T-shirts or bathing suits. And bare feet.

Gulls circled overhead, and the only music was the swooshing of the waves as they rolled onto the shore. Just at eight o'clock, Mom, Emma, Jessie (who cooks and does a ton of other things at the Spindrift), and Mickey's mother and father walked across the beach and sat in the front row. They were followed by Mickey and his brother, the best man, who went to stand on one side of the minister. Then, when Cindy said "Now," I flattened my hair one last time from where the wind had poofed it, tugged at my peach-colored dress, and started across the sand, leading the maid of honor and my sister the bride, who wore a short white dress (and bare feet) and carried an armload of floppy orange and yellow flowers.

The minister said a bunch of prayers and then talked for a while about giving yourself in marriage but not totally giving yourself away. Emma and Mickey's mother even sniffed and dabbed at their eyes. When it was time for the vows, the minister threw her arms out to the sides, and the wind caught her sleeves and made them look like giant white wings. The sun glinted off the tops of the waves as they crested, one after another, and people walking along the beach stopped to watch. And Cindy's and Mickey's voices rang out clearly for everyone to hear.

Afterwards we all went inside the Spindrift for a wedding breakfast, which is different from a regular breakfast because, in addition to the basic muffins and scrambled eggs and sausage, we also had creamed chicken in patty shells and cold salmon. There was punch in a fluted glass bowl with sherbet floating on top, and champagne that Will served in time for the toast. There was a cake heaped high with white icing, with real flowers on the top, and mints and nuts sat in bowls on all the tables. Mom played the piano some, and Mickey's father took a ton of pictures. Then, before we knew it, the party was over, and Cindy and Mickey were outside in Mickey's truck with the tin cans tied on the back, disappearing down the street.

And it was just eleven o'clock in the morning.

When all the guests had gone and everything was cleaned up, Will went off to the post office, Mom headed to Rehoboth to look for a bathing suit, Emma disappeared into her office to do paperwork, and I sat on the porch with Mickey's dog, Bear, who was staying with us. The whole time we sat there, I kept thinking that this was the best and worst day of my life—both at the same time. Best because Cindy and Mickey had gotten married. Worst because now they were gone, and the house seemed emptier than it ever had before.

Cindy and Mickey called that night from North Carolina to thank Mom and Emma for the wedding and the breakfast. Then Mickey got on the phone just to talk to me. "Hey, kidlet," he said. "We'll be back on Friday, and from that moment on I'll be 'big brother extraordinaire.' " Which I took to be French for one of a kind.

The rain stung my face and I jumped up, shaking myself all over and heading for the house. When I got to the porch, I settled into one of the rocking chairs, reaching out to touch the rough shingle wall of the house. The Spindrift is an awesome place just by the edge of the sea and the house itself is large and rambling, and somehow just *being* there makes me feel safe and secure. It has a giant front porch, five rooms upstairs for guests, and a sort of addition stuck on the back for family. There are stained-glass windows going up the stairs and bare wood floors throughout, and the whole house is filled with a clutter of mismatched furniture, with drawers that sometimes stick, and it all smells of the ocean. The word *spindrift* means spray from a rough sea, and I really like the wind-tossed way it sounds.

Though I'd mentioned it to Megan and Tommy earlier, I try not to think about the Spindrift being for sale. Emma put it on the market just after Halloween because, as my grandmother said, she's gotten to the age where she doesn't want all the work and the constant worry about hurricanes and northeasters and the whole place maybe washing out to sea. Emma also said she wants to travel some, and to read all the books she hasn't had a chance to read. Then she laughed and said she knew that—the book part—would never happen.

When Emma told us about selling the Spindrift, I almost freaked out. I mean, the very ground seemed to shift beneath me. "But what are we going to *do*?

Where will we *live*?" I said, once her words began to sink in.

"Well, I don't know exactly," Emma had said. "But somewhere here in town. In Bethany. And we'll all be together—you, your mother, and I."

"But not here? Not at the *Spindrift*?" I wailed.

"Not at the Spindrift, Cassie," said Emma, reaching out to wipe away the tears I didn't know had been rolling down my face. "You know, places are all very good, but it's what's in our heads and hearts that matters most. Sometimes we have to take our places with us, the way a turtle carries his shell."

It didn't help. Emma saying that, I mean. I felt mad and sad and sort of adrift all at the same time. And besides, I wasn't a turtle.

"What about Jessie?" I asked. "What'll happen to her if you sell the Spindrift?" Jessie has worked at the Spindrift for as long as I can remember.

"I've talked it over with Jessie, and she's wanting to slow down a bit. Maybe work on that muffin cookbook she's always talking about."

"And what about Will? What about all the other people who come to the Spindrift year after year? What's going to happen to *them*?"

"You know, I can't imagine anybody buying this big old house unless they plan to use it as a bed-and-breakfast, so I expect Will and everybody else will keep right on coming to the Spindrift, staying in the rooms they've always stayed in," Emma said.

"Yeah, but it won't be the same. It won't be the same at all," I had said as I scrunched down low in my chair and glared at my grandmother, trying to think of a way to save the Spindrift.

Then the Mickey thoughts pushed their way back to the top of my head. "I've got to know for sure if I really saw what I think I saw," I said out loud, getting up and heading for the door. "And if it's true, I've got to make him stop, so things can go back to the way they were before."

I closed the door and leaned against it for a minute. "I can fix this," I whispered. "I *will* fix this."

Three

I WOKE REALLY EARLY the next morning, not sure what it was that I had to do. The rain was steady and heavy and looked as if it would go on all day, and I burrowed down deep in my bed. *Mickey—the party—a girl with a long red braid.* These thoughts swirled through my head as I remembered what I had seen the night before.

No. Mickey wouldn't, I told myself. I shoved my feet to the bottom of the bed, but the sheets were cold, so I curled into a ball again, thinking about my brother-in-law. About how he was special and did things to people, or *for* people. Good things. I mean, he's turned Cindy the Boss and extra-mother-I-didn't-need into Cindy the Okay. Someone I actually want to be with.

He makes my mother laugh.

He engages Emma in these really heated discussions about religion and politics, even though she's told us for years that polite people *never* discuss religion and politics.

He dreams up exotic muffins for Jessie—orange-kiwi-banana or cantaloupe-peach. And she makes them for him.

And as for me, for me Mickey is the big brother I've never had, and a little bit of the father I've never had (on account of mine dying when I was two weeks old), *and* he is the Prince Charming in all the fairy tales I've ever read. Not to mention the fact that he has blue-green eyes and sun-bleached hair. My secret daydream, one that I've never told to anyone—even Megan—is that Mickey had fallen in love with me. Instead of Cindy.

All of a sudden, I knew what I had to do. I pulled myself out of bed, threw on jeans and a shirt, and dug my slicker out of the closet, thinking as I dressed that Mickey ate breakfast every morning with a bunch of friends at the Turtle Café, that he always lingered over a third cup of coffee and was the last to leave. That I would find him there.

Tiptoeing down the steps, I hurried out of the house before anyone else woke up. The wind blew in gusts as I made my way to the center of town. The streets were pretty much deserted, and I didn't have any trouble spotting Mickey's blue-and-yellow truck pulled into the middle of Garfield Parkway. But just to make sure he and his friends were really there, I pressed my face against the window of the café and peered inside. They were. Then I took up my position in the doorway of the newsstand next door, talking to Miss Betty, the owner, and watching the water race along the gutters.

"Everybody's sleeping in this morning," she said. "Haven't hardly sold a handful of papers yet today."

"That's too bad," I said, leaning out in the rain from time to time to check on the door of the Turtle Café.

"Oh, they'll come," she said, moving around in front of the counter to straighten the candy display. "And when they come, they'll buy more than a *Washington Post* or a *Baltimore Sun*, indeed they will. Real rainy-day stuff, magazines, crossword-puzzle books, playing cards, games for the kiddies."

"Yeah, it's the same at the Spindrift. Bad weather's when everybody gets out the picture puzzles, all over the dining-room table."

"You tell your grandmother I've got some new ones in, case she's interested. A right nice-looking pizza, and the Grand Canyon, too."

"I'll tell her."

After that, she went back to her magazine and

I went back to staring at the rain. Soon a bunch of Mickey's friends came out, heading for their cars. I waited for a minute, waved to Miss Betty, and then made a dash for it, hanging on to the heavy glass door to keep it from blowing as I ducked into the Turtle Café.

"Table for one?" the hostess asked.

"No thanks," I said, shaking my head, the water from my hood splattering every which way. "I'm looking for someone." I hurried past her and headed to the back of the restaurant, where Mickey sat alone at a big round table reading the paper.

I stood for a minute, watching the way the lamplight turned his hair a golden yellow. Then I took a deep breath, but before I could say anything, he looked up and saw me.

"Hey, baby cakes, what're you doing out on a morning like this?" he said.

"I need to talk to you," I said, then stopped because I wasn't quite sure how to go on.

"Well, sure. What can I do for you?" he said, getting up and pulling a chair out for me. "Meanwhile, how about the usual? Pancakes?"

"Nu-huh," I said. For as long as I've known him, Mickey and I have had breakfast together at the Turtle Café several times a year. Just the two of us. And we always have pancakes.

The air around me was warm and sweet and suddenly, in spite of myself, I was incredibly hungry.
"Well, maybe. Yes, pancakes, please."

"One order of cakes, one milk, and I'll have a refill
on my coffee," he said to the waitress hovering nearby.

"Lousy weather, huh?" said Mickey.

"I guess," I said, turning to look out the window at
the rain that was still coming down.

"Northeaster," said Mickey.

"Yeah, that's what Emma said last night," I said.

And then we sat, mostly without saying anything,
while I spun the syrup pitcher around and around and
Mickey crinkled the edges of the newspaper. When
the food arrived, I slathered butter between the pancakes and doused them with syrup till they were just
about floating. I cut a wedge, but as soon as I put it
in my mouth I wasn't hungry anymore, and I had to
struggle to swallow it.

"I saw you last night," I said, pushing my plate away
and leaning forward.

"Oh? Where was that? I came into town for an
emergency repair. Customer of mine over on Maplewood had a broken washing machine, no clean sheets,
and a houseful of company arriving before bedtime."

"No. I saw you at a party—on Atlantic Avenue.
Tommy and Megan and I had been up on the boardwalk and we went by there on the way home and

Tommy said, 'Let's go in,' on account of it being a party of people his brother works with and he was even going to be there. Scott, Tommy's brother, I mean. And we did go in, just long enough to get something to eat. And when I went to get the Cokes, that's when I saw you, sort of in the shadows and—"

I caught my breath and kept on going. "And you were with a girl, pulling her close and rubbing her up and down, and I saw you *kiss* her and you've got to stop because—well, because of *everything*."

Mickey let me talk until I ran down, till there was nothing left to say. He played with a dribble of spilled sugar on the table and finally looked up, grinning, and said, "Well, Cassie, you know what they say—that everybody has a double. And you were obviously looking at mine."

"No, Mickey. It was *you*. I saw you. I was at the washtub getting sodas and you were *there*. Just a little ways off."

"Did you call to me?" he asked.

"Yes."

"And did I answer you?"

"No."

"Would I ever not answer you?"

"Well, no, except that last night you—"

"Come on," he said. "Has there ever been a time in all the years you've been my own special little sister that I haven't answered when you called to me? Think about it."

And I did think. About the times Mickey had come to my soccer games and taught me to bodysurf, and once even went to a parent-teacher conference at school when Mom and Emma both had the flu. "No, not up until last night," I said, "but I don't think you heard me and there was music and noise and—"

"Would I have done that to you?" he said, running his fingers through his hair and smiling a humoring kind of a smile. "Would I have done that to Cindy, the about-to-be mother of my child?"

Suddenly I remembered this past Thanksgiving, when, after dinner, Mickey had clinked on his glass and said in a trumpety kind of voice, "Cindy and I are pregnant." I remember how after all the ooohing and aaahing, I had screeched, "An aunt? A baby makes me an aunt?"

"You an aunt and me a papa and Cindy a mama," Mickey had said. "It turns your mom into a granny and Emma into a great-grandma. So what do you think?"

"I think it's cool," I said. "Really cool." I squinted at my sister and thought how she looked softer around the edges already. Maternal, almost. "You look different," I said to her.

"Not as different as she's going to look," Mickey

had said, reaching over and patting Cindy on the stomach. Then he turned to me. "Well, how about it, you going to baby-sit?"

"Some," I said.

"Just kidding. We won't do that to you," Mickey said, cutting himself another piece of pumpkin pie. "We'll all go along as we always have, only now we'll have this terrific kid and you'll be this exalted aunt person. Nothing will change."

And I remembered the funny jangle in Cindy's voice as she said, "You said everything would change, Mickey." But when I looked up to see what she meant, she was busy clearing the table.

"Would I have done that to Cindy," Mickey prodded, "what you seem to think my mysterious double was doing? Answer me that."

And I was back in the Turtle Café, looking at him for a minute. Sure, and not so sure. "It *was* you. I know it was, and Tommy saw you, too. And Megan."

"You're wrong," said Mickey, a sudden edge to his voice. "And what I'd like to know is, are you positive it was *Cokes* you kids were drinking?"

"Of course it was, only we didn't actually drink them because Tommy came and got me and then we left and—"

"You were smart to get out of there, if you ask me," said Mickey, leaning across the table, his fingers close to but not quite touching mine. "Anyway, little bit," he went on, "I don't like to think of you being at a party like that. Sounds like everybody was lots older than you all, and there was probably drinking and lord knows what else going on. I really worry about you, you know, and I should probably tell your mother, but hey, we're friends. And it'll be our little secret. Okay?"

"Okay," I said, my voice small and wobbly. Then I began to feel sick. I jumped up, pushing my chair back and racing through the now crowded restaurant to the front door. Outside, I stopped for a minute to catch my breath before turning toward the ocean and walking into the rain.

Tears and rain ran down my face and into the corners of my mouth. The back of my throat burned and I felt sort of choked up as I leaned on the railing of the boardwalk and watched the waves rise and hang there before pounding against the shore. Foam raced across the beach, then swept back again as another wave came crashing down. The wind whipped the front of my hair, and I yanked my hood down onto my forehead, still staring straight ahead.

Mickey said he wasn't there, I thought.

"Except you saw him," answered a little voice inside my head.

"But he told me he wasn't," I said out loud, beating my fists against the rail. "That's what he said." Just then I sensed that someone had come to stand beside me.

"Cassie? Is that you?"

I turned to see Will in a humongous raincoat that came almost to his ankles and a slouchy hat, water rushing off the brim. "What're you doing here?" I asked.

"Came out to get my *New York Times* and stopped up here to look at the sea."

"It's awesome, isn't it?" I said, meaning the ocean, but also the fact that he had turned up when I really needed someone.

"Definitely awesome," said Will, peering through his water-streaked glasses. "Say, I'm going to get a bite of breakfast at the Dunes coffee shop across the way. Care to join me?"

"Sounds good," I said, suddenly feeling hungry again. And he caught me by the elbow and steered me across the boardwalk and into the coffee shop.

We hung our coats on the backs of our chairs and the water ran off them in rivulets. "How come you're eating breakfast out when you could've had it at the Spindrift?" I said.

"Well, I'll tell you," said Will, opening the plastic-coated menu and pointing. "Sometimes I get a hankering for grits and scrapple, and since Jessie doesn't feature them in *her* kitchen, every once in a while I eat breakfast out. Now, how about you, what'll you have?"

"Not grits and scrapple," I said quickly. *And not pancakes*, I thought. *Never pancakes again.* I ran my finger down the menu and said, "Blueberry waffles, please. And orange juice."

Will gave the orders to the waitress and then we mostly talked about the weather and the end of school and Mrs. Quattlemayer's English class and how I was supposed to be keeping a journal during vacation. It seemed so normal, having breakfast with Will—as if nothing had happened. Our food came, and we ate and talked about what Megan and Tommy and I were going to do this summer, and about Will's grandson Billy in Santa Fe. He told me about the mystery he was working on now and how, in the book, it was the dead of winter and how weird it was every day, when he stopped work, to go outside and find that it was actually *hot*. "Occupational hazard," he said, laughing. "Sometimes the book is more real than the real world."

"That sounds okay to me," I said. "Wish I had a world to pick from that was more real than the one I have now. Where I could fix things and make people do anything I wanted them to do, like characters in a book."

"It often doesn't work that way," said Will. "Sometimes book characters are ornery critters and keep right on doing what *they* want to do, and there's not much the author can do but go along for the ride. Pretty much like life." He propped his elbows on the table, steepling his fingers and staring down into them. "Anything you need to talk about, Cassie?" he said. "I'm not trying to pry, but it's just that when I found you on the boardwalk, you seemed—well, a tad upset."

For a minute I was tempted. For a minute I wanted to take all the Mickey stuff churning through my head and dump it there for Will to help me sort out. But I knew I couldn't tell anyone, even him, what I thought I'd seen.

"That's okay. It's nothing special," I said, shaking my head. "Except—do you think that sometimes people *lie*?"

"Yes," said Will, his voice suddenly grave. "Sometimes some people do. And the thing is, it makes life wretchedly hard for the rest of us."

"And do you believe in doubles, people who look like other people?"

"That I can't help you with. They say it's true—that everybody has a doppelgänger—but I just don't know."

We sat another few minutes without saying anything. Then we got up and gathered our coats, head- ing outside and into the rain.

thing. Then we got up and gathered our coats, heading outside and into the rain.

Breakfast was still going on when we got to the Spindrift. I sat down at the table, listening while Emma told the new people in Ebb Tide the names of some of the restaurants in town. I talked to the Carsons, who come from Philadelphia a couple of times a year, and looked at pictures of their grandchildren, and nodded as the schoolteacher sisters from Virginia said, more or less in unison, "Rain's bound to let up soon."

When they had all finished eating and drifted off, I got up and helped Emma clear the table. Jessie and I had just started to load the dishwasher when Cindy came in, which is something she does a lot. "Lousy weather," she said, hanging her wet slicker on a doorknob and fixing a cup of tea. "And if you ask me, everybody in town's out driving up and down Route 26, looking for what to do in Bethany in the rain." She lowered herself carefully into a chair at the end of the table, resting her arms on her beachball of a belly.

"You feeling all right?" asked Emma.

"Yes, fine. I just came from the doctor and she said, 'Any minute now.' And it can't happen soon enough for me," she said.

"It'll come, sooner or later. Always does," said Jessie. "And how's Mickey holding up?"

"Working hard. Even last night he had to come back into town—somebody's washer was acting up. A real emergency," Cindy said. Something went off in my head, but when I looked over at my sister, she seemed so normal, stirring sugar into her tea, that I told myself things really were okay.

Four

WHEN THE CALL finally came, a couple of days later, Mom and Emma and I all dived for the phone, but Mom won.

"Yes," she said into the receiver. Then "Yes, yes, yes," for maybe a hundred times. "Yes, yes—uh-huh—yes. And you'll let us know?" She hung up the phone and stood staring at it for a minute, in case there was something else, some little afterthought it was going to share with her.

"Cindy and Mickey are leaving for the hospital," she said. As if we hadn't already figured that out.

"What happens now?" I said.

"We wait," said Mom.

"Just wait? Is that all?"

"Babies sometimes take a long time coming," Emma said.

"And meanwhile I'm going to the office," my mother said, picking up her purse from where she'd dropped it when the phone rang.

"Your first grandchild's about to be born and you're going to the *office*?"

"Yes," said Mom. "What else is there *to* do?"

"Well, I don't know, but it seems like there ought to be something," I said as I followed my mother through the kitchen and on out back.

"Mickey's there with Cindy," my mother said. "He'll be timing her contractions and rubbing her back, giving her chips of ice and just keeping her company."

"Is he really? Doing all that stuff, I mean?"

"Of course he is, and he'll be with her right through the delivery, sharing what is probably one of the most special times in a marriage."

Mom had a sort of spacey look on her face, and she sounded so totally sure that I was sure, too. That Mickey would really be there with Cindy doing all those things. That he was still the Mickey I wanted him to be.

"Okay?" said Mom as she got into the car.

"Okay what?" I said, trying to catch up with what else she had said.

"Okay that you'll help Emma around here today, so

when the call does come, she'll be able to go and meet her great-grandchild."

"Okay," I said again, waving as Mom backed her car out of the parking area and headed down the street.

If you ask me, Mickey couldn't have gotten through with a call from the hospital even if he'd wanted to, because of the way Emma and Jessie kept picking up the phone, listening for the dial tone, then hanging up again. "Just checking to make sure it's not out of order," first one and then the other said.

"Did you do that when I was born?" I asked. "Keep testing the phone and all?"

"Well, when you were born I was already living down here, and I had my bag packed and sitting by the back door, ready to go—you'd've thought *I* was the one having the baby," said Emma, launching into the story I never got tired of hearing. "And the minute your daddy called and said he was taking your mother to the hospital, I jumped in my car and started driving to Philadelphia. I'd arranged everything with Jessie ahead of time, about taking care of the Spindrift."

"And then what happened?"

"I arrived just about the time you did and, my, you were a beautiful baby. After that I stayed awhile to take care of Cindy and to help your momma."

"Then you went back home?"

"I went back home and was there only a couple of days—" Emma's face, which was puckery with sun lines and wrinkles, went flat. "And then I got the other call, the one saying that your father had died in a motorcycle accident."

"And you went back to Philadelphia?" I said, urging Emma along with the story.

"Went back till after the service, when I packed you and Cindy and your mother up and brought you down here. It was all we could think to do at the time, with me needing to be in Bethany to tend to the Spindrift. And the funny thing was that it was only supposed to be temporary, till Laurel got on her feet again—"

"Except . . ."

"Except we all fit together like fingers in a glove, and before long your mother got a job at the real estate office, and Jessie and I minded you girls while she was at work. And truth to tell, I wouldn't have had it any other way," said Emma, running her fingers through her short white hair.

"Me neither," I said, trying for a minute to think what it would've been like if Mom and Cindy and I had stayed in Philadelphia and never come to the Spindrift.

"Now, come along," said Emma, breaking into my thoughts. "Let's tend to things around here, so we'll be ready to go over to the hospital as soon as we get the call."

And we did tend to things. I rode my bike down to Shore Foods to get milk and bread and whatever for Emma, so she wouldn't have to take the time to go to the Food Lion out on the highway. Afterwards I changed the sheets in Ebb Tide and Gull's Nest, swept the front porch, and checked on the outside shower. Jessie vacuumed the upstairs, and Emma worked in her office and talked on the phone to a man in New Jersey who tried his best to convince her that the Spindrift's "no pets" policy shouldn't apply to his precious poodle, Phoebe. Which it did, same as it does for *all* pets except Bear, who comes a lot with Cindy and Mickey and is always welcome.

Megan came by after lunch and we took off for the beach, setting down our chairs facing the house so we'd be able to see Emma signal if she had any news.

"I never knew it took so *long* to have a baby," I said, smearing sunblock all over myself. "It was ages ago that Mickey called, when they were leaving for the hospital."

"Do you think it *hurts*? I mean, hurts *a lot*?" said Megan.

"I don't know, but I bet it does. And I wish now that I'd paid more attention at the childbirth class I went to with Cindy, except that they were talking about pain management and sort of boring stuff like that. Anyway, Mickey's there with her, which'll make it all okay." I put my head back and closed my eyes, feeling the sun beating down and listening as the waves rolled against the shore. That swooshing of the waves is one of my all-time favorite sounds, and one of the best things about the Spindrift is that I can hear it from every room in the house.

From somewhere far away, I heard Megan say, "You never told me what happened after the other night, when we saw Mickey at the party with that girl. Did you say anything to your mother?"

The weird thing was, I hadn't let on about going to talk to Mickey at the Turtle Café, though Megan and I mostly told each other everything. I guess because I wanted to believe in Mickey and couldn't take a chance on Megan saying, *"A double? He said it was his double? Get real, Cassie. Believe that one and I'll tell you another."*

"Well? Did you?" she asked. "Say anything to your mother?"

"Nuh-uh," I said, shaking my head. "Anyway, it was sort of dark at that party and it probably wasn't even Mickey—just someone who looked like him." Then quickly, before Megan could say any more, I said, "Do you think childbirth's really the way it was in *Gone*

with the Wind when Melanie was having that baby with
the whole city burning around her?"

"If it is, then I'm not having any kids," said Megan, putting her head back and closing her eyes.

"Me neither," I said. "Unless you had this really fantastic husband and he was right there with you. Maybe then." I sifted sand through my fingers and thought about Mickey at the hospital with Cindy, holding her hand and rubbing her back.

"No word yet?" said Mom when she came in from work a little after five. "I called the hospital this afternoon, and the nurse said, 'Everything is progressing nicely.' Whatever that means."

We ate supper—veggie burgers and sliced tomatoes and potato salad—and watched the news on the little black-and-white TV on the kitchen counter, which Mom never approves of, only tonight didn't seem like a regular night.

We cleaned up the kitchen and then, just as I was reaching into the cupboard for a bag of cookies, the phone rang. We stood there frozen. It rang again and we knew, from the way it sounded all loud and trumpety, that it was *the* call.

"A *girl*?" I shrieked into the phone.

"Yes, a girl," Cindy said again, her voice sounding strong and quivery, both at the same time. "A little girl, only she's eight pounds seven ounces, so she isn't exactly little."

"What's she look like?"

"She's beautiful."

"Beautiful how? What kind of hair does she have? What kind of nose and ears and—"

"Well, she doesn't have a *lot* of hair, but what she has is blond and fuzzy and she looks like Mickey."

"She looks like Mickey," I said, handing the phone to my mother but keeping hold of the cord. All of a sudden I yanked on it, interrupting Mom, who was asking Cindy how things had gone and how she felt, stuff like that. "Her name," I said. "I never asked her name."

"Her name is Erin," my mother said, beaming in a way that let me know she was already totally into this grandmother thing. Then she blinked and her voice sort of caught as she said, "Erin Casswell Taylor."

And suddenly I felt prickly all over on account of the Casswell part, not so much because it was my name, but because it had been my father's. Only everybody called him Caz.

I watched Mom hand the phone to Emma and heard my grandmother say, "Now you give that baby a kiss for me and tell her we'll be there in no time flat. We're leaving now—soon as I call Jessie and tell her the news."

•   •   •

The hospital wasn't exactly around the corner. In fact,
it was in Lewes, another whole town, which is, as
Emma says, three-quarters of an hour away on a good
day—and forty-five minutes any other time. But that
night it seemed as though someone had hold of the
road on the other end and was pulling it out, farther
and farther away. We went past trendy developments
like Cotton Patch Hills and Pelican's Pouch, across
the Indian River Inlet and along the stretch of shore.
We went through Dewey Beach and skirted Rehoboth.

"I thought we'd never get here," said Mom as she
pulled into the parking lot and stopped the car. "Let's
go see the baby."

The maternity section was on the third floor and on
the walls were pictures of storks holding pink and blue
bundles, which was pretty hokey, if you ask me. Everything seemed muffled and tiptoey as we made our way
down the hall to room 314.

Mom knocked and pushed the door open, and there
were Cindy and Mickey, sitting on the bed, eating pizza.
As though it were any old day. *Except*, right next to
them, in a pink-and-white box kind of thing set on a
cart, was the baby. *Their* baby.

I don't quite know what I expected. I mean, we'd
been hearing nothing but baby baby baby for months.
I'd seen the sonogram and gone to a childbirth class

and helped Mickey paint the nursery and once, even, put my hand on Cindy's stomach and felt the baby kick. But I hadn't been prepared for there actually to *be* one. Right next to the pizza crusts. I stood still, holding tight to the door as Mom and Emma moved forward, making twittery noises that didn't sound anything like them.

"Come on, Aunt Cassie, come and meet your niece," said Mickey, catching me by the wrist and pulling me across the room.

"See, I told you she was beautiful," said Cindy, getting out of bed and leaning over the baby. "She really is, don't you think? And I'm not just saying that because she's ours."

I wasn't at all sure about the beautiful part. I mean, this baby was small and scrawny and sort of red, with a fuzz across her head that, I guess, was hair. And she didn't look anything like Mickey.

It didn't matter that I couldn't come up with anything to say, though, because by then Mom, Emma, Cindy, and even the aide who had come in with a pitcher of ice water were all talking at once.

"Where's the camera, Mickey?" asked Cindy, picking up the baby and handing her to my mother while she settled herself back on the bed. "Can you get a picture of the four generations?"

Mom gave the baby back to Cindy and sat on one

side of the bed next to her. Emma sat on the other side.

"Say cheese," said Mickey, backing up to get them in. "Then I'll take another with you all looking at the baby."

I stood watching my family and thinking how, even with Emma's white hair, they all looked alike—small and wiry and as if they were just waiting to get up and *do* something. I thought about Erin Casswell and wondered if she'd take after her mother and grandmother and great-grandmother, or after Mickey, who was medium tall and stocky. Or if maybe she'd be like my father and me and end up *really* tall and have to stand in the back row of all the pictures she was ever in.

"Now one with Cassie, too," my mother said.

"Mickey, you should be in this one, too," Cindy said. "Maybe we could get one of the nurses or somebody to take the picture."

"No, just your family in this one," Mickey said.

"You're our family," said Emma, but Mickey was changing the film in the camera and didn't answer.

When the picture-taking was done, Emma got up and moved to a chair across the room and I slipped into her place, reaching out to touch the baby's finger.

"Want to hold her?" asked Cindy.

"Well, should I? I mean, is it okay to keep, you know, handing her around?"

"Oh, yeah," said Cindy. "Besides, we're bonding—all of us with Erin." She eased the kid into my arms and I sat there, sort of shaking and hoping she wouldn't break and thinking that maybe this aunt business was going to be okay. So long as they didn't ask me to baby-sit too often.

We all stared as Erin Casswell Taylor squinched and unsquinched her mouth and waved one of her tiny fists. After a while, my mother reached for her. "I'll put her back in her bed now because Cindy and Mickey have some presents to open."

I retrieved the shopping bag from where I'd dropped it by the door and put it down on the bed next to Cindy.

"What's this?" my sister asked. "You've already given us presents, the crib and all those things at the shower."

"Yes, but we all agreed we couldn't come to meet Erin empty-handed. Go ahead," said Mom, pointing to the bag.

Then there was a flurry of ribbons and paper as Cindy opened a copy of *Goodnight Moon*, an Aloysius bear, and a pair of yellow overalls that Emma insisted Erin would be into by Christmas. The whole time this was going on, Mickey stood with his arms crossed and his face sort of wooden, as if maybe he was thinking ahead, about Erin and how someday she'd need a bike and jeans and to get her ears pierced. And to go to college.

All of a sudden I wished we'd brought something just for him. Like one of those T-shirts with WORLD'S GREATEST DAD across the front. I could almost see him putting it on and strutting up and down the hospital corridors with Erin in his arms, smiling and bowing as he went. At least, that was what I wanted to see, what I wanted him to be. The World's Greatest Dad, I mean.

Next thing I knew, Emma was standing up and motioning to the rest of us. "Come along. Let's us be off so Cindy can get some rest. Mickey, you go home soon and get yourself a good night's sleep. Tomorrow you'll be taking your family home."

Will was waiting in the kitchen when we got back to the Spindrift. He must have told everybody else about us going off to see the baby, though, because we'd no sooner gotten in the door than the other guests came drifting in—Mr. and Mrs. Carson, the new people in Gull's Nest and Seascape who'd just arrived that afternoon and didn't even know us, *and* the two sisters from Virginia, already in their bathrobes and with their hair rolled tight in pin curls.

They all seemed to be talking at once, and little bits of their conversation spun through the air. *A new baby. A little girl. Lots of pictures.*

Will and Emma served iced tea, and Mom put cookies on a plate.

I stood by the back door, thinking about Cindy and Mickey and Baby Erin, and how, though Mrs. Quattlemayer had suggested we keep a journal this summer, I hadn't actually started one yet. And that I'd have a lot to write tonight.

Five

"I CAN'T BELIEVE we forgot the car seat last night," said Mom the next morning at breakfast. "It's times like this when I really wish you were old enough to have your license, Cassie."

"You and me both," I said, giving the lazy Susan in the middle of the kitchen table a whirl.

"No problem," said Emma. "I have to go over to Lewes this morning anyway, so Cassie can just ride along with me and run the car seat up to Cindy while I'm doing my errands. We'll have it there well before Mickey arrives to take her and the baby home."

"Can Megan go? To see the baby and all?" I asked.

"Probably not a good idea," said Emma. "It's pretty traumatic, getting your first baby ready to go home, and Cindy may be a little anxious. Anyway, Erin will be around for a long time—Megan'll have plenty of opportunity to make her acquaintance."

"I'll pick you up here in forty-five minutes," Emma said as she pulled into the circle in front of the hospital. "I just want to run down to Canal Antiques and take a look at a set of framed quilt squares they called me about. Tell Cindy that your mother will be dropping a pan of lasagna off at the house later, though I guess Laurel already told her that—and don't stay too long."

"Okay, just long enough to deliver the car seat and say hello to Erin," I said, waving and heading inside.

There was a woman on the elevator with an "IT'S A GIRL" balloon and a big grin on her face. "First grandchild," she said, tugging on the string so the balloon bobbled up and down.

"Me too," I said. "Well, not me exactly, but my mom's first grandchild. *My* first niece. She's going home today, and last night with all the excitement we forgot to bring the car seat and apparently she has to have it."

"Oh yes, they're really strict about that. Why, in my day we just held the babies in our arms the whole way home."

Just then, the elevator door slid open and we both stepped out.

The maternity floor was as muffled and tiptoey as I
remembered it from the night before, but as I started
down the hall I heard a rumbling sound, kind of like a
thunderstorm off in the distance. An aide pushing a
cart of sheets and towels stopped and I stopped oppo-
site her, and we raised our eyebrows at each other and
waited for the noise to stop. The rumbling turned into
a roar, though. Someone must have opened a door,
letting words pour out into the hall. Angry, snarling,
spitting words that bounced off the walls and ceiling
and carpeted floor.

"I will—"

"You won't—"

"I can—"

"You can't—"

"Thought things would be better . . . and at a time
like this—"

"Sick of it . . . always checking on me—"

"Get out then—"

"Can't be fast enough—"

And Mickey shot out of Cindy's room, his face an
ugly red, his hands clenched into fists as he ran down
the hall.

"Mickey, no! Wait, where are you going?" I called.

I stepped out in front of him, trying to stop him, but
he kept coming, coming, coming. Like a train on
a track. It was as though he didn't see me until he

crashed into me and sent me flying into the wall, where I slid in a heap onto the floor. And even then he didn't stop. "Mickey, no," I said again, watching as he disappeared down the steps.

The aide knelt beside me, and a nurse who seemed to have appeared out of nowhere kept pushing me back as I tried to get up. "Are you sure you're all right?" she asked. "Did you hit your head?"

I tried to shake my head, but stopped when it hurt. I rubbed at my shoulder. "I'm okay, I think," I said, looking in the direction that Mickey had gone, then down toward Cindy's room. A strange howling noise came from the open door. "That must be Cindy, my sister," I said as I stood up.

"Let's see what we can do for her," the nurse said as she picked up the car seat, took me by the arm, and led me along the hall.

Cindy was crouched against the head of the bed, her arms locked across her stomach. She rocked back and forth and made a noise that was not like anything I'd ever heard before. It was both high and low and sounded as if something really hurt, deep inside of her.

"Cindy," the nurse said. She reached out her hand, but my sister pulled even farther back. Then she saw me.

"What are *you* doing here?" she said.

"I came to bring the car seat. We forgot it last night and—"

"Where's Mom?"

"At work. I rode over with Emma because she had an errand and—"

"Go get her then. Go get Emma. Somebody's got to take us home."

The nurse reached out again, and this time Cindy caught her hand and held it tight as she started to sob.

"Emma is—?" the nurse said to me after a while, sort of mouthing the words over Cindy's head.

"My grandmother," I said.

"Can you get her? If you're sure you're okay."

I nodded and turned for the door, but before I could get there Erin started to cry, too, a thin, wavery cry, and I wondered if she had been frightened by all the noise.

I went along the hall past the nurses' station, down in the elevator, through the front door, and out to the circle where I was supposed to meet Emma, before I realized that only a few minutes had gone by and it would be ages before she got there. I stood for a moment, not sure what to do next, and then turned and, still in a kind of trance, went back inside.

"May I help you?" asked a woman in a rose-colored smock who sat at the information desk reading a magazine. "Do you need to find someone?"

"No, I already found her, my sister, I mean. But

yes"—I swallowed hard, as if that would make the tangle of words come out straight. "I need to make a phone call, only I haven't any money, but it's about my sister, and the nurse upstairs said to get in touch with Emma—she's my grandmother—and get her to come right away because something's happened and Cindy's crying and—"

"Press 9 for an outside line," the woman said, shoving the phone toward me.

I looked at it as if I'd never seen a phone before and said, "But she's not home. She's over at Canal Antiques about the quilt squares and—"

"You need the number," the woman said, taking out a phone book and looking something up before punching in the numbers and handing the receiver to me.

Someone must have answered and I must have said something, because all of a sudden Emma was on the other end saying, "Hello—hello."

"It's me, Cassie, and Cindy needs for you to come right away on account of what's happened, and the nurse said to call and—"

"Cassie, what's wrong? Take it slowly and tell me what's wrong. Is Cindy all right? How about the baby?"

"They're all right, but not *all right*. I mean, when I got upstairs Mickey was already here and he and

Cindy were having a fight—and now Cindy says she needs someone to take her home."

"But what about Mickey?" Emma asked.

"He's gone."

There was a silence that seemed to go on forever. Then Emma said, "I'll be right there."

When I hung up, the woman at the desk was busy with a florist's deliveryman, and I went ahead and called my mother at the office. I told her what I'd told Emma, only a little bit more, about the fight and all. But not how Mickey had looked when he came storming out of Cindy's room, not what he had done to me. And when she said she'd come right away, I told her no, to wait till Emma got there, that we'd call her.

I thought about going back upstairs, but the picture of Cindy crouched on the bed, rocking and making animal noises, gave me cold chills all over. Besides, I told myself, the nurse was with her, and the aide, and maybe a doctor. Instead, I headed out the front door and sat on the curb, staring at the flowers in the circle at the center of the driveway. Suddenly they were too bright and too cheery, and I wanted to tear at them, to rip them up and tell them it wasn't that kind of a day anymore.

The sun beat down on the top of my head and I tried not to see the hard, angry way Mickey's face had looked as he came down the hall toward me.

"What happened?" I whispered, rubbing my shoulder. "What's going on?"

I remembered Mickey the day we met him. Remembered his Mickey-smile and his eyes that were the same greeny-blue of the ocean. He had come to the Spindrift late one summer afternoon because of what Emma called a "plumbing emergency," which meant that the washing machine had gushed water everywhere, while a gazillion dirty sheets and towels sat waiting in baskets on the laundry-room floor. He peered inside the washer, turned the water on and off, took stuff apart, and announced that the pump was broken. He would get a new one and come back tomorrow to put it in.

When he was done, Emma offered him a glass of lemonade and Mickey settled down at the kitchen table, asking about the Spindrift and telling about the business he ran from his house a couple of miles outside town. He told us he took care of a lot of vacation properties, winterizing them and opening them up in spring, and that he put in storm windows and screens and repaired just about anything.

After a while Jessie and Emma went to serve lemonade to the guests gathered on the porch, and Mickey and I kept on talking. It was *real* conversation, as if I *mattered*, and not that fake grownup-to-kid stuff some people talk. He asked me what I was doing on my summer vacation, and I told him about the collection of dead horseshoe crabs Megan and Tommy and I had been storing under Tommy's porch until his mother found out and made us get rid of them. He told me about the time his dog Bear met up with a jellyfish for the first time. I asked him what Bear looked like and where he was and did Mickey ever take him along to make his calls. He wanted to know how I liked Mrs. Scott as a teacher and said that she had been *his* third-grade teacher, too, and I wanted to know if she used to say "Zip your lips" all those years ago. Then we both laughed and tried to talk with our lips zipped.

The next morning Mickey came back with Bear (who was no particular breed but sort of lumbered like a bear) and the new pump to fix the washer. It took him ages, though, because after Megan and Tommy and I had been helping for a while, Cindy came in. All of a sudden my sister had an overwhelming interest in the insides of the washing machine. And Mickey had an overwhelming interest in explaining them to her.

After the washer was done, they went around front and mended the saggy middle step and then sat right down on it and talked till lunchtime, when the two of them headed off to the Turtle Café to talk some more. Emma always said she felt right sorry for the folks who were waiting for the Taylor Home Maintenance Company (aka Mickey) to come and fix something *that* day.

Anyway, from then on, it became *Mickey and Cindy*, same as people say *cream and sugar* or *bacon and eggs*. And the funny thing was, it wasn't just Mickey and Cindy but *Mickey and all of us*. He was a piece of our family.

"Mickey, how could you?" I said again, this time out loud, just as Emma came along the walk from the hospital parking lot.

"What happened?" she asked as soon as she saw me.

"Oh, Emma, it was so terrible. Right when I got here they were having this dreadful fight that everyone could hear, and then Mickey stormed out and Cindy was sort of howling, and the nurse and I went in and that's when she told me to get you, Cindy did. To take them home."

"That must've been upsetting," Emma said, sort of patting me on the head, only I'm taller than she is, so that didn't quite work. "But this is apt to be a tense time for Cindy and Mickey and, well, people *do* have spats, fights even, and everything works out. Why, I'll bet even as we're standing here, Mickey is on his way back to the hospital to get Cindy and the baby."

I stood up, shaking my head, not sure what to say.

"Let's go up," Emma said, heading for the door. "And see what's what."

.   .   .

When we got to the room, Cindy was quiet, leaning back against the pillow with her eyes half closed, the television playing. I was sure she wasn't watching it, though, same as I was sure she wasn't talking to the aide who sat by the bed, making crooning noises to Erin and saying, "Indeed, she is the bestest baby ever, isn't she," over and over.

"Good morning," called Emma from the foot of the bed. "How's my granddaughter this morning? And my great-granddaughter?"

"Oh, Emma," said Cindy, her voice flat, her face all splotched and crumbly. "We have to go home."

"Of course you do—a hospital's no place for anybody," my grandmother went on. "But things are sure to look better when you're back in your own house, with your own things. When Erin's in her nice big crib."

"You don't understand," said Cindy. "We have to go *home. To the Spindrift.*"

"But, dear one," said Emma, pulling a chair up to the bed and sitting down. "I don't want you to do anything hasty. You have your own life now, a husband, a child. Every marriage has its difficulties, problems along the way. You and Mickey—"

"Can we go soon?" said Cindy, getting out of bed and reaching for her clothes. "I just have to take my baby home."

I pressed my back flat against the wall, making my mind go blank and trying not to think.

"Have you talked to your mother?" Emma asked, following Cindy to the bathroom door and still trying to have a regular conversation, as though everything wasn't crashing down around us.

"She called, but she doesn't understand, either. None of you do—none of you ever will. She said we'd talk later, but there's nothing I want to say except that I'm never going to see *him* again."

Cindy closed the door and Emma and I stood there, listening to the sound of running water. My grandmother moved over to the phone, saying, "I'm going to call your mother and tell her that as soon as we get things squared away here, we'll be bringing your sister home."

As for me, I held tight to the edge of the bed to keep myself from pounding on the bathroom door and shouting at my sister, "What'd you do to Mickey to make him act that way? What did you do? He'd never have done that if he'd been married to me."

Six

ALL THE WAY HOME, I kept waiting for Cindy to tell us what had happened to make Mickey act the way he had. She didn't say a word, though, and just sat in the back, next to Erin's car seat, staring out the window and drumming her fingers on the shopping bag of things we'd brought the night before. The drumming got louder and louder, and when I was about to clap my hands over my ears and yell at her to stop, Emma reached out and patted me on the leg. Then she turned on the radio.

Mom was at the Spindrift when we got there, along with Jessie and Will and the Carsons, who were leaving that day and said they needed to talk to Emma about making reservations for later in the summer, but, if you asked me, just wanted to see the baby.

We all stood around for a while, with either nobody talking or everybody talking, in that fake kind of way that people sometimes do. Then I walked outside with Mr. and Mrs. Carson, since my grandmother has this obsession about departing guests being escorted to their cars (it's supposed to make them want to come back), and by the time I got inside again, my life had been rearranged. That quick.

"Don't you think that'll work out, Cassie?" Mom asked, as though I'd been standing there all along.

"Don't I think what'll work out?"

"About the rooms. I was just saying that rather than have Cindy and Erin move back into your room— your and Cindy's *old* room—they can have my room and I'll come in with you. Okay?"

Oh swell. My mother as roommate. My mother, who goes to bed practically with the chickens and who is a natural-born neatness freak, was moving in with me.

"Cassie?" she prodded.

"Sure, fine, whatever," I said, hoping she'd think the sound of me grinding my teeth was really the fan in the corner.

"Well, that's settled, then," said Emma. "Now let's have some lunch."

Jessie sort of pushed Cindy into the big old rocking

chair, handing Erin to her and saying, "Now you go
ahead and give this baby *her* lunch while the rest of us
tend to things around here."

Right away, Cindy did some floppy action with a little blanket over her shoulder and down her front, and
I realized that under all that she was feeding the baby.
Breast-feeding her. Right there in public, for all the
world to see. I mean, I always thought breast-feeding
was okay and healthy and sort of real, but my very own
sister? And in the *kitchen*? Before I could decide where
to look, Jessie handed me bread to thaw in the mi-
crowave, and Mom got busy setting the table, Emma
pulling lunch stuff out of the fridge.

As soon as she was done, Cindy put Erin in her car
seat on the counter and we all sat down, turning the
lazy Susan and helping ourselves to bread and turkey
and sliced tomatoes, to mustard and mayo and, for me,
peanut butter. In between we stared at the baskets
hanging from the ceiling and the duck decoys lined
along the ledge as though we'd never seen them before. And the great conspiracy of silence settled over
us.

I kept waiting for someone to say something. For
Mom to ask what was going on, or Emma to want to
know what had happened this morning. Or even for
Jessie—who usually speaks up only when she thinks

she has something important to say—to, well, speak up.

I guess we were all waiting for Cindy to talk, but she just sat there, staring straight ahead and tearing her sandwich into shreds. We might have sat like that all afternoon, except that at some point Megan and Tommy knocked on the back door.

"Hi, everybody, we've come to drag Cassie off to the beach," said Tommy.

"Cindy! You're here!" shrieked Megan. "And this is the baby! Oh, she's so adorable—and just perfect."

"Yeah," said Tommy, peering down at Erin and dangling his sunglasses over her face. "But she's awful little."

"Hold on, you guys. I'll be with you in a minute," I said as I grabbed my dishes from the table and shoved them in the dishwasher before heading to my room to change into my bathing suit.

"Babies are so cute," said Megan when the three of us were on the beach in front of the Spindrift. "But how come they came to your house? I thought your mom was going over to Cindy's to help. With the kid and all."

"She was," I said, and then, while I coated my legs with sunscreen, I told the two of them what had happened this morning at the hospital. "And now she's here and nobody's asking any questions. And Cindy's not talking."

"That's heavy stuff," said Tommy, peeling off his T-shirt and flopping down on the sand, not even on a towel. Which is a habit of his I find truly disgusting.

"Yeah," I said, shaking my head, "really heavy."

"Do you think this had anything to do with what we saw at the party the other night?" asked Megan.

I held my breath, sort of flattening down what I didn't want to know. "The other night never happened," I said finally.

"Excuse me?" said Megan.

"Didn't happen the way we thought it did, I mean."

"And how do you know that?" asked Tommy.

"Mickey told me," I said. "The morning after that party, I went to see him at the Turtle Café and he told me so."

"Oh, okay," said Tommy, digging himself deeper into the sand. "Mickey has pronounced that it never was—what you saw. Right?"

"That's the point. I didn't really *see* it—him— Mickey, I mean."

"What about what Megan and I saw? Was that a ghost?"

"That's exactly why I didn't tell you guys before. I knew how you'd react. But that night I just saw someone who looked like him—Mickey said it must have been. Everybody has a double somewhere in the world," I said.

"Sure, Cassie," said Megan. "In the world, maybe, like Timbuktu or someplace, but *two* Mickey Taylors right here in little Bethany—"

"And we never noticed," added Tommy.

"That's what he said, and I believe him," I said, pushing my heels down into the sand and telling myself I really did believe. Then, I pulled off my T-shirt and, almost without thinking, rubbed my shoulder, which had turned a funky purplish blue. "But it *was* Mickey this morning, at the hospital."

"Did *he* do that to you?" said Megan, leaning forward and tracing the outline of the bruise with a sandy finger. "Did he?"

"Well, he did, but not really. Not on purpose, I mean."

"What happened?" said Tommy, shooting up out of the sand. "You said he and Cindy had a fight but—"

I sighed and said, "Yeah, that's right. They were having this horrendous fight, and next thing I knew Mickey came charging down the hall. What I didn't tell you, though, was that I got in front of him to try and stop him and he didn't see me and just smashed into me and I hit the wall and fell." I still didn't mention that he had just kept on going. Hadn't even stopped to see if I was okay.

"Did you tell your mother?" asked Megan.

"About the fight, but not, you know, the fall. And promise me—both of you—that you won't either."

"But poor Cindy," said Megan. "You don't think he ever hurt her, do you?"

"No way. Mickey wouldn't do that."

Just then I saw my mother coming toward us across the beach. "Remember, you promised," I said, grabbing my T-shirt and putting it on.

"Sorry, Cassie, but I need you to come on an errand with me," my mother said. "If we hurry, you can get back before the lifeguards go off duty."

"But Mom, why right this minute? And anyway, where?"

"I'll explain on the way," she said. "Now come along, please."

"But I can't—I'm all glopped up with sunscreen."

"That's okay. You have a T-shirt on."

"But *Mom*, we were just—"

"Mary Casswell, *now*," my mother said, turning and starting back to the house.

I rolled my eyes at Tommy and Megan. "See you later," I said, picking up my towel and going after her.

"So what's the mysterious errand?" I asked as we

went around the side of the house and I stopped to hose off my feet. "Where are we going?"

"I have to ride out to Cindy's place and get some clothes for her and the baby, and I'd like you to come with me."

"Mom, no. I mean, what if Mickey's there? What if—"

"I just called and nobody's there. I got the machine."

"What if he comes while we're there?"

"What if he does? What's the big deal?" said Mom. "We're just going to pick up your sister's clothes and diapers for Erin, her little shirts and gowns, and the bassinet, maybe the swing. Now come on, the sooner we go, the sooner we can get back."

The big deal was that after the way he'd acted this morning, I wasn't sure I wanted to take a chance on seeing Mickey. I couldn't, or wouldn't, say that to my mother, though, so I slid my feet into my flip-flops and gave it one last shot. "Why don't you go and I'll just stay here and—"

"Look, this day's been bad enough without you giving me a hard time," said Mom. "Now, I have to go on out there, and I need you to go with me because you've spent a lot more time than I have at Cindy's, and you'll know where to find everything. Besides, I could use a little moral support."

"The baby stuff is in the nursery and Cindy's is in her room, so you just go in and get what—"

"Come on, Cassie. And stop being difficult," said Mom, turning toward the car.

I tossed my beach towel up over the line, wondering how all of a sudden *I* had turned into the difficult one.

I dragged after my mother getting out of the car and going into Cindy and Mickey's house. I dragged after her all the way up the stairs, and once we were at the top I stood in the tiny hall, flipping the lid of the wicker clothes hamper up and down, up and down.

"Come on, give me a hand here," said Mom, heading into the baby's room. "Don't make this any harder than it has to be."

"Me?" I said. "Why am I the one making it hard? Why am I the one—"

"You're not. I'm sorry. It's just that things are so—" Mom's face looked streaked with worry as she started taking baby clothes out of the drawers and putting them in a plastic bag.

I watched her for a minute and then reached out and touched one of the yellow walls, remembering.

It had been a Saturday in late March when I came out here to help Mickey paint the nursery. The week before, he had done doors and windows and baseboards, and he assured me the walls would be the easy part.

After lunch, Cindy and Mickey and I went upstairs, and he handed me a roller and showed me how to use it, which was basically that you just *did*. Backward and forward and every which way. When we were ready to work, Mickey opened a can of paint that was an amazing shade of yellow—more like a daisy than a dandelion, and not at all like lemons or egg yolks or even goldenrod.

Then, almost as if he'd heard a drumroll in the background, he picked up a narrow brush, dipped it into the paint, and drew a humongous heart across one wall. Inside it, he wrote *Mickey loves Cindy*.

Cindy grabbed the brush, dipped it, and added *Cindy loves Mickey* under what he had written.

They stood for a minute, looking at what they had done, until Mickey took the brush again and swirled it through the paint. I closed my eyes, hoping more than anything that he was going to write *Mickey loves Cassie*. I opened them and read *We both love Aunt Cassie*.

My face burned a little and I turned away as Mickey chased Cindy out of the room, telling her to go enjoy being the Queen Bee while the drones did the work. He was right about the walls being easy. They were. We worked the rest of the afternoon, till the daylight disappeared, and I liked the way the roller seemed to whisper as I pushed it up and down. And once we were

done, it really *was* like standing in the middle of a giant daisy.

That warm yellow-daisy glow had stayed with me,
at least till Mickey and I went out to pick up Chinese
carryout for supper that night. There was something,
a twingy deep-down feeling I tried not to think about
that had to do with the sort of smarmy, flirty, oozy way
that Mickey was talking to the girl behind the counter
in the restaurant. I told myself it didn't matter, that he
was just being funny, but the whole thing made my
skin crawl. And when we got back to the house, all I
could do was pick at my Vegetarian Delight.

"We can pile these things in the bassinet and leave
the crib here for when Erin gets bigger," my mother
said, her voice pulling me back to the present. I moved
over to help her take the white skirt off the bassinet.
Then we folded its legs underneath and brought it out
into the hall. From there we went into Cindy and
Mickey's room, moving around the unmade bed, stepping over his clothes strewn across the floor, dirty
glasses and empty cartons of Chinese carryout and
two pairs of chopsticks. The ceiling fan swung lazily,
swoosh, swoosh, swoosh. And for a minute I stood
there, looking all around.

"Okay," said Mom, checking her list. "We need
shorts and T-shirts, underwear, that sort of baggy

denim jumper, tennis shoes, and a couple of extra nightshirts. Cindy said you'd know where to find them, so you get those things together while I check the bathroom for the hair dryer." I yanked clothes out of the closet and the bureau drawers and was just starting around the bed to get Cindy's book off the nightstand when I saw something on the floor. A red-and-white polka-dot bikini.

For a minute, nothing registered. I picked up the book and started out of the room. Then I turned back and nudged the bathing suit with my foot. I closed my eyes and saw Cindy the way she had looked the day before yesterday. Ripe and round, enormously pregnant. And I knew, sure as anything, that if my sister even owned a bikini, she hadn't been able to get into it for a long, long time. I wanted to throw up.

"Ready, Cassie?" my mother called, and I heard her coming toward me. Without stopping to think, I dived for the bikini, shoving it into the carryout bag and stuffing the whole thing into the trash can. I straightened up and was rubbing my hand hard against my shirt when Mom came in.

"What was that?" she said.

"Nothing much," I said, surprised that I could answer her without gagging. "I was just trying to clean up a bit."

"Don't worry with that now," said Mom. "This place

is beginning to spook me a little, so let's get out of here."

In the hall, we piled the rest of the stuff into the bassinet, and with me going backward, we worked our way down the steps and outside. We loaded everything into the trunk, then got into the car.

"Wait," I said, before my mother could start the motor. "What do you think happened—with Cindy and Mickey, I mean?"

"I don't know," said Mom, resting her head on the steering wheel for a moment. "But I'm sure Cindy will tell us what she wants us to know—in her own good time."

Seven

CINDY'S OWN GOOD TIME might have taken forever if it hadn't been for Edna Wilkerson from Smyrna, Delaware, who arrived after supper that night.

"Call me Edna, cause that's my name," she said in a gargly kind of voice when Emma brought her out to the porch to show her where breakfast would be served, and where Cindy and I were hanging out, just rocking back and forth and letting Erin hear the sound of the ocean.

"And you are—?" she said, waggling a knobby finger at the two of us.

"Ah, these are my granddaughters—Cindy and Cassie. And *this* is my great-granddaughter, Erin," Emma said.

"Hmmmm," said Edna, coming close and peering down at Erin. "Doesn't cry, does she?"

"Well, she's a baby—and babies cry. After all, it *is* her first night home from the hospital. I don't think you'll be disturbed, though," said Emma, "because your room is upstairs and—"

"Wasn't worried about that. Not much in this world that can keep Edna Wilkerson awake, certainly not this little sprout here." She nodded toward Cindy and went on, "Came home for a little R and R, did you? A little TLC? Well, I did the same thing when my son was born—went home to Mama."

"And we're thrilled to have them," my grandmother said, heading toward the door and looking back over her shoulder to see if Edna was coming.

Which she wasn't. She shook her finger at Cindy again and said, "Don't stay away too long, missy. I'm sure your husband wants his little family home. Right? You *do* have a husband, don't you?"

"Well, yes," Cindy answered.

"Good. Glad to hear it. Can't be too sure these days," said Edna, starting to follow Emma inside. "Makes me really watch what I say."

"If this is what she's like when she's *watching*, what's she like when she's *not*?" I asked as the screen door swung shut behind them. I rolled my eyes and pushed against the railing with my feet, sending my rocker jolting backward. "That's the one weird thing about living in a bed-and-breakfast. I mean, most of the guests are really nice, but every once in a while we get a complete loser. Can you *believe* her?"

Instead of answering me, Cindy stood up carefully, her face a stony mask. She clutched hold of Erin and went inside.

"Wait!" I said, hurrying after her. But she kept on going, as if walking in her sleep.

"See—it's started already," Cindy was saying when I got to the kitchen. "People wanting to know how long I'm staying, when I'm going home."

"Who? What people?" asked Mom, looking up from the paper.

"Her. That witch. That Edna Wilkerson."

"Who on earth is Edna Wilkerson and what'd she say?" asked Mom.

"The new woman in Gull's Nest—she took the Carsons' place—and she was pretty unbelievable," I said.

"Well," said Mom, taking the baby from Cindy and putting her in the car seat, "that's not *people*, that's one fairly disagreeable woman, from the sound of her. Anyway, it's not to do with her or with anyone else. This is between you and—"

"It's what you're all thinking, I know it is. What you're all saying behind my—"

"Cindy, please. You've just had a baby. You're tired. There's a fair amount of stress." Mom put her hand on Cindy's arm and kept it there until my sister jerked away.

"*Stress*? Is that what you think this is all about—*stress*? I can handle stress. This is about more than stress. It's about all the cheating and lying and sleazing around that I'm not going to put up with anymore. It's about how I'm finally done telling myself that things'll get better, when any fool can see they won't. And I'm not a fool. Not anymore."

I looked up to see Emma and Will standing in the doorway, and I started to slither toward them, figuring the three of us could disappear and leave my mother to deal with what I didn't want to hear.

"No," said Cindy, catching me by the arm. "I want you all to hear this, especially you, Cassie, because of the way that all these years you've thought Mickey was so great. Because of the way you used to look at him with those big sappy eyes. Because you told me once that he'd turned us into a *real* family, whatever that is."

"Yes, but he—"

"But then, every one of you thought he was the greatest, didn't you? The perfect son, the perfect grandson, the perfect big brother. Ever since we got married, he's been the prince and I've been the lucky one. Lucky Cindy to be a part of the perfect couple, when all the time—"

Cindy's face was sharp and hard and streaked with dried-up tears. "Maybe it *is* stressful to have a baby, but I'll tell you one thing—it's plenty stressful not to know which woman that baby's father'll carry on with next. Who he'll be running around with *this* time. When he'll be home. Where he is.

"And then when we found out I was pregnant, he promised me." Her voice cracked, but she went on. "He said that from now on things would be different, that he'd change, we'd be a family."

I bit down hard on my lip and stared at the ceiling fan to keep from seeing him the way I had seen him the other night, pulling the red-haired girl close and grinding his body against hers.

"Go on, Cassie, say it," said Cindy, her voice jerking me back. "I know what you're thinking. 'Not Mickey, never Mickey.' Well, do you want to know what your wonderful brother-in-law did last night—after he left the hospital—do you want to know?" She was beginning to rock back and forth. "Do you?"

I shook my head, but she went on anyway. "I'll tell you what he did. He met up with some woman—this year's tramp. And he took her home—to our house, to our bed, *my* bed, and she spent the night."

Suddenly I saw the room the way I'd seen it this

afternoon—the unmade bed, the empty carton of Chinese food, and the red-and-white bikini on the floor.

Cindy went on, like a top that couldn't stop spinning. "And when I called this morning to ask him to bring me a clean shirt when he came to pick us up, she answered the phone. And I was so naïve and so stupid that I thought I had the wrong number, only I asked for Mickey anyway and she said, 'Okay.' But then when I said I was his wife, she hung up.

"And when Mickey got to the hospital, he didn't even bother to deny it. He said he was tired of sneaking around, that he'd met somebody else, and, besides, he wasn't ready to be tied down." Cindy let go of the edge of the kitchen table and sort of folded herself onto a chair. "Now do you see why I'm here? Now do you see why I can't go back?"

After everybody went to bed that night, I slipped out onto the porch, curling myself into a rocking chair and wrapping a sweater around my knees. I mean, I couldn't go to bed, not with Mom in my room making those little huffy snuffling noises she makes when she sleeps.

The breeze off the ocean picked up and I scrunched down lower in my chair, trying to stretch my sweater to cover the rest of me and remembering the time just after Cindy and Mickey were married when we had all gone out to dinner in Fenwick Island. Mickey had been sitting at one end of the table, and I'd looked at him and said, over the din of the restaurant, "With Mickey here, we look real now. Like a real family." Everybody had laughed. And Mickey had blown me a kiss.

Other thoughts crowded in, and I remembered the Christmas after Cindy and Mickey had met, when he gave her an engagement ring. It was a beautiful glittery diamond, and when Cindy held out her hand to show us, both she and Mickey seemed to sparkle more than the ring. I wondered if that one perfect moment had been what Mrs. Quattlemayer called the hook, drawing us into the Cindy-and-Mickey story.

I remembered another, not-so-perfect moment from that same Christmas—Mom and Emma looking at each other over Cindy's head, talking, the way grownups sometimes do, without saying anything out loud. "I know what you're thinking," Cindy had said. "That I'm too young and I haven't finished college. I know college is important, but marrying Mickey is *more* important. Don't you *see*?"

Then I thought of my sister and the way she looked so alone and yet so strong, standing there in the kitchen tonight, telling her story.

And I thought about Mickey with his sun-streaked

hair and that funny quirky smile that always made me feel as though I was the only person around, even in a roomful of people.

I thought about Cindy again.

My head hurt from thinking, and a part of me wanted to run inside and tell Mom, or Emma, or maybe even Cindy, about seeing Mickey and some girl at that party and how they had been sort of pawing each other. Another part of me knew I never would. Not in a million years. Because if I never told, I could still work at convincing myself that none of this was true.

Eight

"Do you have any idea how much space a baby takes up?" It was a Saturday morning about two weeks after Erin was born, and Megan and I were hanging out at the boardwalk, where we had been watching the aerobics class. After the group disbanded, we stayed put, settling back on a bench to check out the passing scene.

"No, but you're going to tell me," said Megan.

"Hey, that's what friends are for. To listen, I mean. Remember the time you had to go with your mother to help take care of your grandmother after her operation, and there was nothing for you to do and you used to call me every night and complain how bored you were. Until your mother found out you were making all those long-distance calls.

"Anyway, it's a ton. Of space. The family part of the Spindrift is ready to burst, and the weird thing is, I can't figure out why, because for my whole life Emma and Mom and Cindy and I lived there without falling all over each other. And Erin's really little and hardly even takes up any room. I guess it's the *stuff*—the bassinet, the swing, the seat, the stroller, the baby toys and pacifiers that seem to multiply and sprout all over the house, plus all the shirts and gowns and bibs and millions of diapers piled up *everywhere*."

I stopped for a minute to catch my breath before starting again. "That's why I take off every morning after I get the porch set up for breakfast. Why some days I tag along with Will for his constitutionals or stop by the bakery to visit with Tommy. Why you and I've spent so much time watching sweaty women do step aerobics."

"So how's it going today?" asked Megan.

I let out a sigh, trying to figure out where to begin. "Well, first of all, there's my sister, who's back to being Cindy the Boss when she's not into her silent suffering or let's-trash-Mickey mode. And the thing is, she seems to float from one to the other without any warning. Mostly I try to stay out of her way.

"And now my mom's forever on my case to 'be more sympathetic to your sister.' Then the other night Emma and I walked down to TCBY to get frozen yogurt. Afterward we went up to the boardwalk and sat on one of the benches by the bandstand and watched a bunch of kids dance around the stage—the way we used to do when we were little, only we were *good*— but before we got up to leave, she slid into one of those this-is-a-difficult-time-and-we're-counting-on-you talks. And even Jessie got into the act yesterday, when she clucked her tongue at me and said, 'Talk pretty, Cassie. Talk pretty.'

"And the thing is, at times I sort of know I'm being a pain, and just when I work up to changing, Cindy says, Do this, or Mom says, Stop that, or Erin cries, or oh, anything." The sun was hot and I wiped the sweat off my face with the back of my hand. "So that's the story of my life."

"What else is new?" said Megan, pulling her hair up off her neck and twisting it into a ponytail.

"Well, I never said it was *new*—more sort of ongoing. And part of the time I have this total guilt for feeling the way I do about Cindy and the baby being at the Spindrift, and part of the time I can't help thinking about Mickey. I mean, he *is* Erin's father and who's going to be there to tell her the good stuff about him?"

"And *you* still want to believe in him," said Megan.

"Huh?"

"Mickey. You still want to believe in him. It's the

same as it was in English class this year, when you kept arguing with Mrs. Quattlemayer and telling her that Shakespeare should have written *Romeo and Juliet* with a *happy* ending."

"Well, he should've."

"But he didn't—that would have been a different story," said Megan. "Same as, if Mickey was the way you thought he was, he'd be a different person."

"Easy enough for you to say, and now I guess you're on my mother's side. And Emma's and Jessie's."

"I'm not on anybody's side," said Megan. "I just feel sorry for Cindy, is all."

"Yeah, I do, too, but it's such a hodgepodge in my head. I mean, I know what Cindy says, but I still want Mickey back in her life, in all our lives. I still want him to come and take her home and make everything the way it's supposed to be. I still want to be able to fix it." I stood up, peeling my T-shirt away from my body and trying to fan myself. "It's too hot just sitting here, and anyway, I have to go. I've got stuff to do for Emma."

All the way home, I was up to my eyeballs in good intentions. I resolved, from then on, to baby-sit for Erin some and to really help Cindy and maybe even make her laugh again.

Inside, I smiled at Emma and Jessie, kicking off my

flip-flops and wondering if they noticed the new me. I leaned over my grandmother's shoulder to check on the crossword puzzle she was doing.

"You missed the big news," Emma said. "I had an announcement this morning, but you were up and out so early—"

"What news? What announcement?" I asked.

"I've found buyers for the Spindrift—or, actually, they've found me," said Emma. "I got the call from the realtor first thing this morning."

"Somebody's going to buy the Spindrift? They *can't*. Anyway, who *are* they?"

"The Carsons. You know the Carsons. The best part of all is that they've been coming to the Spindrift for years and really love the place. And they want to run a bed-and-breakfast now that they've retired." Emma went on in a perfectly normal voice, as if everything weren't hideously and positively coming apart around us. "They've made a good offer, and I'll feel much better leaving the Spindrift in the hands of people I've known for so long."

"But they can't. You can't *let* them. Besides, that's not an announcement, that's a disaster." I pushed myself away from the kitchen wall and out the door, heading down the hall toward the back of the house.

"Cassie, wait—come back—" I heard Emma calling, but I didn't stop.

My bedroom door was closed and I hit it at a run, slamming it back against the wall. Just then Cindy appeared out of nowhere, hissing and shushing like an angry goose. "Don't go in there, Cassie. Come out of there right now."

"What are you talking about?" I said, turning to face her. "This *is* my room, at least it was the last time I looked, though you never know around here."

"But Erin's in there sleeping, and I don't want her to wake up just yet."

I blinked and blinked again as I saw the bassinet between the two beds. "What's she doing here? Isn't one room enough for you? Now you need two?"

"Shhhh, lower your voice," whispered Cindy. "She's been fussy all morning and I needed to vacuum my room, so I put her in here while I did it. No big deal."

"Not to you maybe," I said. "But it's a big deal to me."

"Sorry," said Cindy. "And isn't *someone* in a good mood today."

"I was in a fine mood until I came back here and—"

"But didn't Emma tell you the news?"

"You mean, the *disaster*? Of course she told me—she said—"

"Did she tell you all the news?" my sister asked.

"She told me *enough*, though I guess it doesn't matter to *you*. The Spindrift doesn't matter to you—or anything else. Not Mickey or your house or Bear or Erin having a father. You've ruined everything, and if you ask me, whatever made Mickey do what he did is all your fault." I hurled myself into the room and onto the bed, clamping my hands over my ears and trying not to hear the sound of Erin crying or the squeak of the bassinet wheels as Cindy moved it out of the room.

I heard Cindy close the door and I lay there, my face pressed against the spread, not caring about the heat or the sweat running down my neck. *The Spindrift has been sold.* The words ran through my head like a tape that never ended. *The Spindrift has been sold.*

I thought about the Carsons and how, up till now, I'd always figured they were perfectly nice, normal people. If I'd known, I would've *done* something, I told myself. Like telling them there was a Spindrift ghost, or that the pipes clanked in winter and sometimes broke. And that, during storms, the wind howled around the corners of the house and might one day blow it clear away.

After a while I rolled over and stared up at the ceiling and thought about the Spindrift. I recited the names of the guest rooms—*Sandpiper, Rose Room, Gull's Nest, Ebb Tide, Seascape*—as I pictured the stained-glass windows on the stair wall and the giant linen press at the end of the second-floor hall, where Megan and

Tommy and I used to play hide-and-seek when we were little. About my secret hiding place in the hot and dusty attic and my all-time favorite place on the downstairs porch. And the sound of waves as they hit the shore.

Jessie knocked on the door and called in, saying, "Tommy's on the phone and wants you to play volleyball." I told her to tell him no. She knocked again to say that lunch was ready, and I said I wasn't hungry.

Sometime later, I got up and put on a bathing suit, stopping by the empty kitchen just long enough to grab an apple before heading for the beach. I ate half the apple before I realized I didn't want it, and tossed the rest away, watching as two gulls attacked it.

I dropped my towel, waved to the lifeguard, and raced into the ocean, letting the waves beat against me. Catching my breath, I dived under one and then another, and another. I pounded the water with my fists, saying, "That's for Mickey." "For Cindy." "For me because I trusted them and thought everything was so great." "And that's for the Carsons on account of they don't have any *right* to buy the Spindrift." When I couldn't fight anymore, I let a giant wave wash over me, carrying me forward and grinding me into the sand, dumping me on the shore, where Will, in his baggy yellow bathing suit that hung to just above his knobby knees, stood waiting for me.

"You going in the water?" I asked, standing up and pushing my hair out of my eyes.

"Not right this minute. I just thought we'd walk a bit," said Will.

"Walk? Now?"

"Just up a ways and back again," he said, setting off to the north and assuming I would follow him. Which I did.

We walked on the hard, wet sand, stepping around kids building castles and digging for fiddler crabs. Every once in a while, I looked over my shoulder at the trail of footprints, Will's long and spidery and mine just sort of solid.

"You see, Cassie," said Will after we had walked a bit, "I find I'm having a hard time standing by and watching you make your grandmother unhappy."

My skin felt prickly and my shoulders tightened. Will seemed to know that, because the next thing he said was, "Now, don't go turning into a porcupine on me. Just hear me out. Do you have any idea how happy Emma is to have found buyers for the Spindrift? What good news that was for her?"

We stopped walking and turned to face the ocean. I dug my toes into the sand. "I think I *do* know, deep down. It's just that I don't want the Spindrift to be sold. I want to go on living here forever. But I didn't mean to hurt Emma. I didn't—"

"Think of the relief it will be for her not to have to worry every time a hurricane or even a good strong northeaster heads this way. Think of—" He stopped for a minute and shook his head. "I don't mean to sound like a Dutch uncle here," he said in a way that let me know there was lots more he *wanted* to say. "And I know I'm not your grandfather or—"

"I never had one of those, or a Dutch uncle either. I never had a father," I said, tracing a giant circle in the sand with my big toe.

"You had a good strong mother, though," said Will. "And a good strong grandmother. You had Cindy."

"Then we got Mickey," I went on. "And now he's gone, and nothing's the same as it used to be."

"That's the ongoing process we call life," said Will in a voice that sounded both abrupt and kind at the same time. "And part of that process you didn't give Emma a chance to tell you about this morning is that she and I have decided to get married."

"*Married?*" I shrieked. People walking by and even swimmers as far out as the breakers turned to look at us. "You and Emma are getting *married*?"

Will nodded, his face a sudden pinky red that I was pretty sure wasn't sunburn. "And I, for one, am accepting congratulations."

"Well, yeah, that's cool," I said as we turned and started back. "That's more than cool." We walked in silence until I said, "And that means you'll be here all the time now? At the Spindrift?"

"I'll be in *Bethany* all the time," Will corrected me. "With Emma and with the rest of you."

"But not at the Spindrift—because it's being sold." I said the words slowly, feeling the way they stung. "Well, Bethany. That's what I meant to say."

When we got back in front of the Spindrift, Will turned and headed into the surf. "I'm going to have that swim now," he said. "But, Cassie, when you go inside, give your grandmother a hug. And while you're at it, cut your sister some slack."

After he left, I sat down on the wet sand, scooping and shaping and shoring up the sides of an abandoned castle that had been partly washed out to sea. I watched Will's head bobbing out past the breakers, and then I got up and headed to the house.

Nine

I DID GIVE EMMA a big hug. But there wasn't a lot I could do about Cindy—wasn't a lot I actually *wanted* to do. Partly, I guess, because she was avoiding me as much as I was avoiding her. When I was in the kitchen, Cindy was in the dining room. When she was on the porch, I was in the living room, picking out "Heart and Soul" on the piano.

Even when Jessie made one of her special carrot cakes and all the guests assembled after supper for an impromptu party to celebrate Will and Emma's engagement—even then, Cindy and I managed to be in different places at the same time. It gave me a creepy feeling, but later that night, when I tried to write in my journal about Cindy, it was Mickey I ended up concentrating on. She was my sister but he was—well, Mickey.

The next morning I was out early, and for once I didn't go by the bakery to see Tommy or stop and pick up Megan or even wait for Will. I stayed away from the boardwalk and the aerobics class, heading instead for the side streets and going up one and down another. Up and down, as though I was searching for something but didn't know what. Some of the time I looked at houses and tried to imagine living in them. Some of the time I willed the Carsons to change their minds and not want to buy the Spindrift, though I was pretty sure that wasn't going to be. And in what was left over, I thought about Will and Emma and the way Will blushed when he told me they were getting married and how, last night at the party, they reached out from time to time to touch each other's fingers. When they thought no one was looking.

I had just started down Third Street when I saw Mickey pull up in front of a weathered gray house. I ducked behind a crape-myrtle tree and watched as he took his toolbox from the back of the pickup, said goodbye to Bear, and headed inside. I waited a minute to make sure he hadn't forgotten anything, then ran over to the back of the truck, throwing my arms around Bear and letting the big dog slobber all over me. "I've *missed* you," I said into his fur. "I've missed so many things." Tears stung my eyes, and I rubbed at them with one hand, holding tight to Bear with the other.

Bear looked at me with his big dark eyes and then leaned forward, resting his head on my shoulder in a comforting way that let me know he understood. Having a part interest in Bear, which Mickey gave me the day he and Cindy got engaged, had sort of made up for not being able to have a dog at the Spindrift. (Because, as Emma explained, not everybody likes dogs, and some people are even allergic. If you ask me, *they* should just stay home, or go to a hotel.)

I stood there for a while, scratching Bear behind one ear and thinking about Emma and Will getting engaged and how the Spindrift was being sold and that we were going to have to move. I heard Mickey coming out of the house, calling over his shoulder, "Any more trouble with that dryer, you let me know, okay?"

Then, because it seemed like the thing to do, I ran around to the side of the truck and yanked the door open, sliding onto the seat, scrunching down low and jamming my knees up against the dashboard and closing my eyes.

I heard a *thunk* as the toolbox landed in the back, heard the driver's side door open and Mickey get in. "You don't give up, do you, kid," he said, starting the engine.

I opened my eyes and waited until he had pulled out onto Route 1 and was heading up the highway, away from town. "But you said you didn't do it," I said.

"You said I didn't see you at that party. You said it was your double—that everybody has one—and besides, that you would never—"

"I lied," said Mickey.

His words fell like stones. "You *lied*?" I said.

"Look, drop it, will you? That morning at the Turtle Café—hey, I told you what you wanted to hear. Now just let it go. Last thing I need is any more interference. Any more—"

"But how about the things you said at the wedding?" I asked. "How about 'for better or for worse' and 'in sickness or in health' and 'for richer or for poorer'? How about *those*?"

"How about 'em?" said Mickey as we bounced along past stumpy bushes and scrub grass.

"Why *did* you? Say all that?"

Instead of answering me, he swung the truck to the right, into a development, and, checking a pad on the dashboard for the address, pulled up in front of a house with about a million porches. Without saying anything, he got out and took his tools from the back of the truck.

I stared after him, mouthing the words, "Why did you?" Then I let my head fall back and listened to the cry of a gull. After a while, the truck grew hot and steamy and my legs stuck to the plastic seat and made a sucking noise when I went to lift them. I opened my door and got out, moving around to the back of the truck to visit with Bear.

As I stood there, I watched a boy shooting baskets at a house across the street, giving him three points for every ball he got in and taking away two for every one he missed. *Three, six, nine, twelve, ten, thirteen, eleven, fourteen, seventeen.* I kept score in my head.

I counted mailboxes on posts up and down the street and spindles on the porches of the house Mickey was in. I was thirsty and looked around for an outside spigot, but I didn't want to go too far from the truck, so I gave up.

A man holding a toddler came out of the house next door, followed by a woman carrying a string bag filled with buckets and shovels. They put the child down and, each holding on to a hand, started walking slowly toward the beach. I watched till they disappeared over the dune and, even then, kept staring after them. For a minute I pretended they were Cindy and Mickey and baby Erin.

I got back in the truck and closed my eyes, watching the squiggles on the inside of my lids, and kept them closed until I heard the door open and Mickey get in beside me. "Had enough? Want to keep going?" he said as he slammed the truck into gear and pulled out onto the highway, still heading north.

I started to panic, wondering how far he was going

and what I would do if he didn't turn around soon, how I would get home again. I wondered if I really wanted to be alone with him. Then I squashed those thoughts, shoved my fingers under my legs, and got on with what I had to say. "I want you to make it all okay again. I want you to take Cindy and Erin home and—"

"Did your sister put you up to this? Did she?"

"No," I said, hating the way my voice sounded all small and wobbly. "I just want you to—"

"And I don't give a hoot what you want. Got it? I don't want to make it 'all okay.' " Mickey slipped a cassette into the tape player. "Look, kid, stop messing with things that don't concern you and get it through your head that for once in your life you can't be Little Miss Fixit."

I cringed when he said that, because Little Miss Fixit was one of the things Mickey used to call me, but in a nice way and not all mean and sneering as he was now.

"But what about *Erin*?" I said, reaching out to cut the volume so that Billy Joel's voice turned into a whisper. "You haven't seen her since that day at the hospital and she's grown and gotten even prettier."

"Yeah, I'd like to see her. I'll get over there one of these days," said Mickey. "But the idea of a kid still

freaks me out, so I guess I'm not ready for this father
bit. I'm not sure I'm ready for the husband bit, either:
there's a whole big world out there and a lot of women
in it."

"What do you mean, *not ready*? You *are* a husband.
And now you're a *father*, too."

"What can I say except get off my case, Cassie. I just
told you—this isn't to do with you, and stop trying to
make me into something I'm not." He slowed the
truck and turned into Cotton Patch Hills, stopping in
front of a blue house with a white railing.

It was then that rockets seemed to explode inside
my head. "It *is* to do with me cause that's my *sister*
you're talking about!" I screamed. "That's Cindy. And
I'm *glad* she brought Erin and came home. I'm *glad*
she left you because you're nothing but a lying, cheating scumbag, a dirtball lowlife. She's a hundred million times too good for you. And everything you've
ever done is fake. All of it. Every bit."

I pushed the door open and got out, slamming it behind me. Just as I started to move off, I caught myself
and came back, holding on to the truck, leaning into
the window and shouting, "And another thing, Mickey
Taylor, I'm glad I finally know what you're really like.
I'm glad, glad, *glad*."

I turned away from him, blinking at the sunlight

and feeling the heat press down around me. Then, trying not to think about how far I was from town, I started for the highway.

I waited ages for a break in the traffic, while, one after another, cars swooshed past me, leaving blasts of hot air behind. As soon as I got the chance, I dashed as far as the median strip, and then the rest of the way across, curling my toes and praying that my flip-flops didn't go flying off. Stopping a minute to catch my breath, I started to walk, all the while watching the shoulder of the road stretching ahead, and turning back to check on the cars bearing down on me from the rear. It was then that I realized I should have stayed on the other side of the highway. That I should have been facing the traffic. Suddenly the road looked miles wide, though, and I didn't even think about crossing back.

I walked quickly in the beginning, thinking Sousa marches in my head and planning to set some kind of record between Cotton Patch Hills and home. The heat seemed to swell around me, clogging my throat, and I felt myself moving more and more slowly. Sweat trickled down my chest. I pulled my T-shirt away from my body and tried to cool myself, but it didn't work. The sun burned my face, my arms, my legs, and I felt hungry and thirsty and half sick all at the same time. I counted the steps between telephone poles and wondered why I got a different number every time. I stopped to dig out a stone that was wedged into the rubber of my left flip-flop. I thought about Mickey and hoped he wouldn't come after me, but when I turned to look over my shoulder, everything blurred and I felt dizzy.

"How many miles to Babylon?" I recited out loud. "How many miles to Bethany Beach?" *Three . . . four . . . five . . . six . . . seven . . .* I didn't want to know—and I did. Was I halfway there yet? I thought about hitchhiking, about stopping and holding out my thumb and waiting until somebody picked me up. I actually turned around, but before I could do the thumb bit, years of Mom's and Emma's and Jessie's warnings came crashing down around me. "No hitchhiking ever . . . No getting in cars with strangers . . . Never, never, never . . ."

I faced forward again and kept going.

> *How many miles to Babylon?*
> *Threescore miles and ten.*
> *Can I get there by candlelight?*
> *Yes, and back again.*

And finally, after all that, I let myself think about Cindy.

Ten

I THOUGHT ABOUT HOW I'd yelled at Cindy and told her that whatever Mickey had done, it was all *her* fault. About the way she had howled in the hospital after he left, and how she'd stared into space the whole way home, and how even now her voice sometimes sounded flat and empty when she spoke.

I thought about the girl at the party with Mickey and wondered who she was. I wanted to get hold of her and shake her till her teeth fell out, even though I knew it wouldn't do any good. I thought about Mickey and the way his creepy-crawly hands were all over her, and about the red-and-white bikini in his and Cindy's room, and how at first he'd said he had a double and then he'd said, "I lied." Right out. Not even caring.

I thought about how what I'd said to Mickey was

true: that he *was* a lying, cheating scumbag. A dirtball.
A lowlife. And how all the times I'd told myself I believed him I'd been lying, too. To myself.

I thought about how he'd stolen something not only from my sister but from Mom and Emma and me as well.

Just thinking this made me feel caved in and raw, as if something big was suddenly missing. Then, like an ant trying to move a stone, I forced my thoughts back to Cindy—and what I could do for her. Not getting Mickey back or wanting to make everything okay—I'd tried that, and it hadn't worked—but what I could do to make up for what I'd already done and said.

It seemed as if I'd been walking forever when I stopped and turned to check on the cars coming up behind me, half hoping that someone I knew would pull over and give me a ride the rest of the way home. Then, one at a time, I took off my flip-flops, rubbing each foot and brushing the sand from between my toes. I did a couple of deep knee bends and thought of sitting down by the side of the road. But, as tired as I was, I didn't relish being roadkill, so I stayed upright—and, I hoped, visible. I swung my arms, but the sun had burned and tightened the skin, so I stopped that in a hurry. I took a deep breath just as a truck went by, and I almost choked on the rank-smelling air.

I started walking again, trying out in my head scenarios to maybe use on Cindy. When I gave Emma a hug the other day, after Will and I had talked, she seemed to know all the things I wanted to say and hugged me back. But if I hugged Cindy, she'd probably barf. All of a sudden, I remembered an old movie Megan and I had watched on TV once—a kind of soppy love story where the message was, if you love someone, it means you never have to say you're sorry.

The trouble with that was, I was pretty sure it wasn't true. The message, I mean. I was pretty sure that if you loved someone, you *did* have to say you were sorry. I was also pretty sure that, somewhere way deep down, I loved Cindy. In a weird, sisterish way. So I knew what I had to do, but just thinking about it made me feel cold and clammy. Even though the sun was blazing.

I looked up and saw that I was in front of the antique store on the edge of town. I was almost home and I started to walk faster, counting out my steps. *One. Two. Three. Four. Five.* A horn blared in back of me. It blared again as my mother pulled alongside me.

"Where have you been?" she called, leaning out the window. The little worry lines around her eyes were white against her sunburn, and her mouth was flat and straight. "Do you know that I had to come home from work because Emma called and said that nobody had seen you since you took off this morning? Do you know that we've called Megan and Tommy and anybody else we could think of and that I've been all over this town? Get in the car right this minute."

I got in, dropping my head back on the seat and stretching my legs out under the dashboard. It was obvious, by the way Mom was going on, that she had been really upset. But all I could do right then was let her words wash over me.

"And look at you, you're burned to a crisp. And maybe even dehydrated. Here, drink this," she said, pulling a water bottle out of her bag and handing it to me as she started the car. "But not all at once—just a little bit at a time."

I took a swallow and then another. I spilled water on my chest, and it felt so good that I pulled the neck of my T-shirt out and poured some more there on purpose.

"It's not like you, Cassie, to go off like that for such a long time without checking in. It's totally irresponsible. I mean, Bethany's a nice, safe town, but the world is full of weirdos, and you just never know. Not in this day and age. And Emma has been positively frantic, staying there by the phone while Will and Jessie scoured the boardwalk and I drove up one street and down the next. Do you know we were within *minutes* of calling the police. You just better have a good excuse, young lady. You better have a darn good excuse," my mother said as she pulled up behind the Spindrift.

The world was waiting inside. Emma and Cindy and Will and Jessie, even Megan and Tommy and Megan's mother, all the guests from the bed-and-breakfast, including the New Jersey couple who were checking out this morning. And they were all talking at once.

"Here she is now—"

"Where'd you find her—"

"Been looking everywhere—"

"Worried out of our minds—"

"Somebody get a wet paper towel for her face. Look how red she is—"

I stood in the middle of everybody, shaking my head and saying, "It's okay, I'm okay. I didn't mean for you all to—It's just that—"

"All's well that ends well, I always say."

Gradually the voices faded as the guests drifted away. I saw Mrs. Mallonee steering Megan and Tommy toward the back door, saw Megan mouth the words "Call me" as she left.

"Now, suppose you tell us where you've been," my mother said.

"I don't see what the big deal is," I said, collapsing at the kitchen table. "I just went for a walk."

"Walk? What kind of walk was that?" said Cindy.

"I don't think you have any idea how worried we

were," said Emma, pouring a glass of orange juice and putting it in front of me. "When you didn't come home after a reasonable time, I called Megan and Tommy, and when they hadn't seen you, I called your mother. The world's not as safe a place as it used to be."

"Lot of fretting going on around here," said Jessie.

"And then there's that ocean," said Emma. "I wasn't sure but what you'd gone for an early swim and—"

"You thought I'd *drowned*? Just because I took a little bit longer walk than usual and lost track of time?" I looked at the clock over the door and was shocked to see it was well after noon.

"We were worried," said Mom, sitting down beside me. "And sometimes when people worry they tend to overreact. But even so, it was an inconsiderate thing to do."

"Walk *where*?" said Cindy.

"On the highway."

"Who walks on the highway in flip-flops?" she asked.

And then, because I felt tired and beaten down, I said, "I was with Mickey."

The room was suddenly choked with silence. After what seemed a long time, Will said, "Mickey?"

"How'd you get with Mickey?" my mother asked.

"I saw his truck in town, and when I heard him

coming I hid inside, and then he got in and headed up the highway, on account of that's where his calls were. And finally I got out and walked home."

"But I don't understand," said Mom. "Why did you get in Mickey's truck? And why didn't he drive you home?"

"I didn't want to ride with him anymore, I never would've," I said as tears welled up in my eyes. "And that's all I can say because now I need to talk to Cindy."

Talk about the Great American Vanishing Act. All of a sudden Will and Emma were gone, Jessie was gone, Mom was gone, and it was just Cindy and me alone in the kitchen. And she was making me a peanut-butter-and-jelly sandwich.

"Are you okay?" she asked, setting the plate down on the table and rooting in the refrigerator for a Coke. "What were you doing with him, in the first place?" She sat down across from me.

I tried to speak, but my throat was stuck together with peanut butter and I swallowed hard. "I'm sorry," I croaked. "I'm sorry for saying what I did about what happened with Mickey being all your fault and for not believing you and believing *him* and for wanting things to go back to being how they used to be cause I liked our family better with him *in* it and for being really dumb about a lot of things and sometimes think- ing you're a pain."

"Sometimes I am a pain," said Cindy. "And don't ever say you're dumb." She played with the saltshaker on the lazy Susan, sliding it in circles around the sugar bowl. "That's the thing about Mickey—it's what he does best—the way he spins a kind of magic, drawing you in tighter and tighter, so that once you find out what he's *really* like, it's almost impossible to believe it. Or to break away."

"Did he? With you?" I asked, biting into the second half of my sandwich.

"Did he ever," said Cindy. "He smooth-talked me up one side and down the other, but I have to admit I went willingly, and with my eyes open."

"What do you mean?"

"I mean, I knew and I didn't know—what Mickey was like. I'd heard all the stories, but managed to convince myself that once we were married he would change. He wouldn't pull that kind of stuff on *me*. I listened to Mom when she tried to talk to me, but didn't hear a word she said. I—"

"*Mom?* Mom knew?" I said. "Except for thinking you were too young, I always thought she liked Mickey. She laughed at his jokes and—"

"Everybody laughs at Mickey's jokes, and everybody

likes him until they get to the point where they can't stand him. Only I guess it took me longer than most." Cindy sat back and ran her fingers through her hair before going on. "I thought it was okay in the beginning, but I was wrong. And then when we found out about the baby, he swore to me that he was going to change. That he was finally ready to be a husband and a father. But that morning in the hospital, when I discovered that nothing had really changed, I knew I had to get out. I realized I was able to do for Erin what I'd never been able to do for myself. If that makes sense."

"Sure," I said.

Cindy leaned forward, looking at me carefully. "I still think he should have brought you home."

"No," I said, shaking my head. "I didn't want him to. Wouldn't have let him, on account of I told him he was a lowlife scumbag and got out and slammed the door. I *wanted* to walk."

"Oh, Cassie, I'm sorry," Cindy said. "Same as I'm sorry you had to find out what Mickey was really like. I know—I've always known—how important he was to you."

I put my head down for a minute, then looked up and said, "I need to know something. He never hit you, did he? He never hurt you?"

Cindy shook her head. "No," she said. "Mickey's not a monster—but he's not a grownup either, and he doesn't really care about other people. And I know now that Erin and I are better off without him."

The phone rang, and in another part of the house, someone answered it. I heard the sound of the vacuum cleaner, and a car horn from out on the street. "It's weird, and I never thought I'd say this, but I guess I'm glad that you and Erin came to the Spindrift. And not to your other house."

"I think that morning in the hospital I didn't want to go anywhere near what you call my other house. Besides, that was Mickey's house from before we were married and it's where he's had his business, so legally it probably won't be counted as belonging to *both* of us." She got up, clearing the table and giving me a lopsided smile. "I guess that means you're stuck with me—you and Mom and Emma and Will. Wherever we all end up."

Eleven

DON'T GET ME WRONG. I mean, the Spindrift didn't suddenly turn into something out of the Brady Bunch. Cindy and I didn't become Jan and Marcia, giving each other those simpering smiles and tossing our hair back over our shoulders for emphasis, as if either one of us had enough hair *to* toss. Cindy was still her same old self—and sometimes a pain. I was still me—and sometimes a pain right back. Just not as much so. Either of us.

For example, there was the time she said in her most Cindyish voice, "Take that diaper out to the trash right now, Cassie. You *could* help around here." And I said, "Take it yourself." And after a while she said, "Please." And after another while I said, "Okay."

Every so often, we even did things for each other:

beyond-the-call-of-duty things. Like the time I changed
one of Erin's poopy and totally and grossly disgusting
diapers all on my own. And the time Megan and
Tommy and I desperately wanted to go to the movies,
only there was no one to take us and pick us up. And
Cindy did.

The rest of July slipped by and suddenly it was Au-
gust. The produce stands out on the highway were
overflowing with cantaloupes and peaches and tomatoes. New people arrived at the Spindrift, stayed
awhile, and left. Will went to Santa Fe to visit his family for a week and then came back again. Megan and I
still hung out at the boardwalk in the morning, and
once we even paid to rent a step and join the aerobics
class, but we ended up laughing so hard we had to quit.

Erin grew and started sleeping more during the
night. She learned to coo and to catch hold of her
toes, though Jessie said that was just by accident. Mom
and Emma and Will looked at houses.

And my sister went to see a lawyer about getting a
divorce. She left one morning, with Erin in the car
seat. When Emma offered to baby-sit, Cindy said,
"Thanks, but no thanks. This concerns the two of us
and I want her to be there." Which, if you ask me, was
bizarre. I mean, of all the places I figured it was important for Erin to go—the beach and the boardwalk
and the bandstand where the concerts are—a lawyer's

office in Georgetown, Delaware, was never one of them.

My mother had taken the day off because, as she put it, "It's been a busy season, and I could use a day at the beach." In all the years I've known her, my mother's never taken time off *just* to go to the beach, and it was obvious to the rest of us that she wanted to be there when Cindy got home. To maybe pick up the pieces.

But when Cindy got home, there didn't seem to be any pieces to pick up. I'm not sure what I expected, a lot of sniveling and snuffling I guess, but when my sister came in, she looked pretty much all together. Like she'd been to the library, or even the Food Lion.

Then, as if she really *had* been to the library or the Food Lion, we all sat down to lunch. Partway through, Jessie reached for a pickle and said, "How'd it go this morning at that lawyer's office? He help you out?"

"He was a she," said Cindy. "And it went pretty well. I mean, it was horrible, and right in the beginning I wanted to grab Erin and run, but then, in a bit, it seemed okay to be there. I guess, because after all these years of not knowing what to do, I was finally doing *something*.

"I liked her—the lawyer. Her name is Anne, and it's good to have someone on my side."

"We're on your side," I blurted out, trying not to think of all the times I hadn't been.

"I mean, in a legal way. She said she'll talk to

Mickey's lawyer and try to work out support for Erin, and for me in the beginning. They'll work out visitation rights for Mickey, too. She's really tough, but not just with Mickey—with me, too. Says I'll have to see about going back to school, that I'll have to learn to support myself. It's scary."

"It's very scary," said Mom. "But you know you can do it, don't you? You know we'll be right here to help you."

"I know," said Cindy, sighing. "It's just that I still can't believe what Mickey did to me. And to Erin."

And to me, I thought, staring down at my empty yogurt cup. *What he did to me.*

"I've got it all figured out," I announced one Tuesday morning when Megan, Tommy, and I were sitting on the edge of the basketball court trying to decide if it was too hot to shoot a few baskets.

"Not Mickey again," said Tommy.

"Not Mickey," I said, letting out a giant sigh and thinking how everything that had happened with Mickey was history. "It's about saving the Spindrift and finding a way for Cindy to support Erin and all that stuff. Listen, this is a great idea. Mom and Cindy can take over running the Spindrift. When Emma and Will are married, she can move into his room upstairs. And everything can go along pretty much the way it's always been. Right?"

"Wrong," said Tommy, scooping up a ball with his foot and catching it. "What about the people who've already agreed to buy the Spindrift?"

"The Carsons?" I said. "Well, Emma'd have to tell them she's changed her mind."

"Doesn't work that way. My dad's in business and I know for sure that there're things like contracts, and it's the law that you have to do what they say."

"Yeah, well, I'll bet if Emma called them up and just explained—"

"Dream on," said Tommy, getting up and tossing the ball to Megan. "Meanwhile, the two of us'll play a little one-on-one."

I slouched down low on the bench, staring at the toes of my tennis shoes, looking into the future and thinking of the way it could be. I saw Mom in what used to be Emma's office, doing paperwork, and Cindy greeting guests and showing them to their rooms. I saw Jessie still concocting these really fabulous muffins. And I saw Erin, a big girl, helping me set up for breakfast on the porch, or in the dining room in rainy weather.

I was all set to present my fabulous idea that night at supper, especially since Will and Emma had gone to Rehoboth, and it would just be Mom and Cindy and

me. Except that Erin fussed. All during the meal. And
nothing seemed to help, not walking or bouncing or
burping or singing.

"Put her in the Snugli, Cindy, and we'll all go up to
the boardwalk and get ice cream," said Mom. "I'm
sure the motion of your body and the cool ocean air
will put her right to sleep. You're coming too, aren't
you, Cassie?"

"I guess," I said, because even though it's considered
basically dorky to go to the boardwalk at night with
your mother and sister and baby niece, I knew I was
going to go anyway. I had something to say and was
waiting for a chance to say it.

We stopped first at TCBY for frozen yogurt and
then went on to the boardwalk, standing at the back
end of the crowd and listening to the band play music
that was loud and wheezy. And definitely uncool. Almost as soon as we got there, everybody started into a
sing-along: "Yankee Doodle," "The Old Gray Mare,"
and "Bicycle Built for Two." That was when I slith-
ered off into the shadows, leaning on the rail and
looking out to sea, hoping that if any kids from school
saw me they'd think I was just hanging out. By myself.

"Mom's looking for you, Cassie," said Cindy, coming up behind me. "Now that the concert's over, she
wants to talk to us. She's by the bandstand." I followed

my sister, settling down on the bench where Mom was sitting, and propping my feet on the one in front. "What's up?" I said.

"I thought we should talk," my mother said.

"But can I go first? I have this terrific idea that will work for all of us and I've been bursting to tell you about it. You and Cindy."

"Okay," said Mom. "What's it about?"

"About how we don't have to move at all. About how you and Cindy can take over running the Spindrift, and Emma can move into the Sandpiper with Will, and Cindy can have Emma's old room and you can go back to *your* room and we won't be crowded anymore, and then Erin can grow up with the sound of the waves always in the background, and as she gets older she can learn to help with the B and B the way I always did, and life can just go on. The way it was meant to be."

Mom was shaking her head even before I finished talking. "It won't work, Cassie. I'm sorry," she said.

"Why not?"

"Oh, a lot of reasons." I waited, and after a while my mother went on. "First of all, there are the Carsons and Emma's agreement to sell the Spindrift to them. She'd never go back on that, even if we wanted her to. Then there's my job."

"You could give it up. That's the point. And run the Spindrift. You and Cindy."

"But I *like* the real estate business—and I'm good at it—and I don't want to run a bed-and-breakfast any more than I think your sister wants to."

"Emma was really into it," Cindy said. "She loved meeting all the people and greeting them and having them come back year after year. I'm not sure what I'm going to study when I go back to college, but it's not going to be this."

"And besides," said Mom, "we'd have all the worries that Emma's always had about storms and hurricanes and wondering what was going to happen next."

"So that's it?" I said, feeling pretty much like a balloon with the air fizzling out. "It's just decided, like that? My idea doesn't even get a vote? How about a democracy—and being *fair*?"

Mom gave me a half smile that was supposed to let me know she understood. "I'm sorry, Cass. But sometimes life just—"

"And don't tell me again that life just isn't fair," I said, squashing my yogurt cup into a chocolatey mess. "Or that when I get to be a grownup, then I can make the decisions."

She didn't. Tell me again, except I'd heard it so often in the past I pretty much knew that that was the rule. We sat there awhile without saying any more, till finally Mom took a let's-get-this-over-with breath and said, "While we're more or less on the subject, I need to talk to you about where we're going to live."

"What do you *mean*, where we're going to live?" I asked.

"Emma said we'd all be together," said Cindy. "That she'd get a house big enough for the six of us."

"That's the point," said Mom, taking off her glasses and putting them away before going on. "I think it's time for the four of *us* to get a house of our own. To let Will and Emma get their own place."

"A house of our own?" I said, suddenly sitting up straight. "We've always lived with Emma, and I don't see why we can't just go on, even if it can't be the Spindrift. Only now Will will be with us, too."

Mom shook her head. "When your dad died, just after you were born, Cassie, my mother took the three of us in and helped me pull myself back together. And because it was working well for all of us, we just stayed put." She shook her head again. "But now it's time."

"For what?" I said, poking Cindy in the ribs and hoping she'd say something. But she just sat there, folding and unfolding the strap of the Snugli.

"For us to move on," my mother said. "To let Emma and Will move on. Anyway, they want to do some traveling, so maybe a condo would be better for

them now. And besides, all newlyweds need to be on
their own. Don't you agree?"

Cindy nodded, and I said, "Newlyweds? They're
too *old* to be newlyweds."

"You can be a newlywed in your sixties, same as you
can in your twenties," my mother said, reaching over
and wiping something off my face that could have
been a tear, but I wasn't sure. "Let's give them a
chance to be on their own."

"But Emma *loves* us. She wants to be *with* us," I said.

"And she will be with us. There's just about no place
in Bethany that's farther than ten minutes away from
any other place."

"I think Mom's right," said Cindy the traitor.

I bit down hard on my bottom lip and waited a moment. "You think she's right?" I said finally. "How
come?"

"I don't know—I just do," said Cindy, shivering
slightly. "It's romantic, and besides, newlyweds *should*
be on their own." She wrapped her arms around the
Snugli and pulled Erin even closer.

I took a deep breath and turned to my mother.
"Where would we live, then?" I asked.

"I've been going through listings at work and there
are several places for sale that look promising, especially one. It's about a quarter of a mile back from
Route 1, with three regular-size bedrooms and one

rather small one that would be for Erin, and the house itself is set right in the middle of a stand of pines. How about we go look at it tomorrow?"

Mom and Cindy began talking about bathrooms and counter space in the kitchen and a screened porch in back and about how Jessie would probably be willing to baby-sit for Erin when Cindy was at school, but I only half listened, concentrating instead on the row of paint blisters on the bench in front of me. We sat there till Erin started to squirm inside her Snugli and Cindy stood up. "Come on, let's go. I want to get her home before she has to be fed."

I trailed after my mother and my sister as they started up the boardwalk, not really caring who saw me now.

"Hey, Cassie." I looked over to see Megan and Tommy and a bunch of kids from school calling to me from down on the beach. "We're getting up a game of volleyball—come on."

I stopped, looking back at them. I felt bruised, sort of all over, and not really together. Just then Tommy hurled the ball in my direction and I reached out and grabbed it. "Yeah, okay. I guess," I said, starting for the steps.

Twelve

MEGAN AND TOMMY and their parents sat in the third row at the wedding, behind Cindy and Erin and Jessie and me. We were behind Emma and Will and Mom and Will's son Frank from Santa Fe. It was a Saturday in late September, and we were all (including Miss Betty from the newsstand, Will's grandson Billy and the rest of the family, a bunch of friends, and even the guests from the Spindrift) in the little shingle church on Maplewood Street, waiting for things to begin.

A man in a yellow shirt played sort of wandering music on the organ, the air conditioner hummed, and, in back of me, Megan cleared her throat in a way that meant for me to turn around. Before I could do it, though, a door opened and the lady minister came in—the same one who had married Cindy and

Mickey—in what looked like the same white robe, only this time she had her shoes on.

The minister went to the front of the church and turned around, holding her arms out, drawing us all in. "I want to talk to you today about trust and faith and a friendship that blossomed into love," she began.

I thought about Will and Emma and how they talked about things and asked each other questions about the puzzles, and how she read his chapters once they were done, and how they held hands walking on the beach.

"Emma and Will, as you take a giant step into the future, we want you to know that we share your happiness, that we . . ." The minister's voice was singsongy and sort of low, and I found myself drifting off, thinking instead about the grandfather I had never known and about Will's first wife, who had died a long time ago. I wondered if they were together someplace, watching this wedding today, maybe on direct-from-heaven satellite TV or something.

I remembered that other wedding, on the beach in front of the Spindrift, and how it hadn't been the beginning of a fairy tale, after all. I thought about Mickey and how he wasn't the kind of person I had wanted him to be. And how I hated what he had done and never wanted to see him again, and had even managed to be out when he and his parents came to see

Erin last week. I knew he was her father, and no matter what he'd said about the idea of a kid freaking him out, it looked as if he was going to be part of her life. Which was good, I guess. I mean, I wanted Erin to know the magic side of Mickey, and I crossed my fingers and hoped she'd never have to know the other side.

I thought about Cindy and how I was sure, deep down, that she'd be okay.

And I thought about the house Mom had bought, which we were going to move into soon and which was actually an okay house even though it wasn't the Spindrift. And how even though it wasn't on the ocean, it was surrounded by pine trees that seemed to whisper when the wind stirred through them.

I thought about school and how I had Mrs. Quattlemayer for English again this year and how, though she said she wasn't going to ask to see our journals, she was already after us to observe—and to *write, write, write*. And how, almost for certain, I was going to try out for a part in the chorus of the school musical, even though it meant singing a solo for the audition. And I thought about Terry Waddell, who sits behind me in homeroom and twice already has walked me to math class.

But most of all I thought about Will and how he had been waiting for me when I came into the kitchen this morning. "Walk?" he said, holding open the screen door and sort of bowing. We went up Pennsylvania Avenue to Sea Colony, talking about the September sky and how nice it was that most of the crowds were gone. We watched the ducks for a few minutes, and just as we were about to leave, Will caught my hand in his gnarled, spotted one. "I love your grandmother, Cassie, and I will never disappoint her. Or you either. I promise you that this is going to be a *good* marriage."

"I know," I said, and the funny thing was that I *did* know. He let go of my hand and we started home, not saying any more but wrapped all around in that comfortable kind of silence.

Just then Emma and Mom and Will and Frank got up and moved to stand in front of the minister. It was sort of surreal, seeing them there like that, and even more so seeing my mother and grandmother in dresses and the men in suits. I mean, this was Bethany, where even when people dressed up they didn't *really* dress up.

I heard the minister saying, "Do you, Emma, take Will for your lawful wedded husband, to have and to hold, in sickness and in health, from this day forward, so long as you both shall live?" All the words sounded new again, and special, and as if they really mattered and would go on mattering.

I heard Emma say, "I do," her voice soft but clear.

I heard Will say, "I do," when it was his turn.

And I felt tingly all over because I knew, from the way their voices sounded, that they were talking only to each other. That, just for a minute, the rest of us were extra. Then the little organ rang out, something loud and trilling, and my grandmother and my new grandfather turned to face us, his arm around her shoulder. And we all started to clap.

As we headed out of the church, I dug a Kleenex out of my pocket and quickly rubbed at my eyes. "Hey, you got allergies, too?" Will's grandson Billy said.

"Yeah," I said. "You want a Kleenex?"

There were caterers back at the Spindrift because Will wanted a bang-up party without him or Emma or Jessie or Mom or Cindy or me having to do any work. That suited everybody just fine, except maybe for Jessie, who snorted a bit and said that she could whip up a wedding reception fit for a king with one hand tied behind her back. "I don't doubt it for a minute," Will had said. "But though I'm marrying a queen, I myself am just an ordinary guy, so I guess we'll settle for a store-bought party."

Waitresses scooted all over the first floor of the Spindrift with trays of mushrooms stuffed with crab, with scallops and shrimp and a couple of things I didn't know the names of and couldn't pronounce once they told me. They also had veggie stuff that Will had ordered especially for me.

"Fabulous," said Megan as we stood in the dining room, staring at a mountain of fruit and waiting for a man in a chef's hat to serve her slivers of beef on crusty French bread. "This is really fabulous."

We filled our plates and headed for the porch, cutting through the living room, where we spotted Billy wedged on the couch between his parents and looking bored. "Come on," I called, nodding toward the door, and he jumped up and followed us, stopping only to grab a handful of shrimp from a passing waiter.

We found space at a table on the corner of the porch where Jessie was telling a group of guests from the Spindrift about the time she was written up in the newspaper. "They called me the *muffin maven*, and the photographer who came to take my picture said I ought to write a book. Wanted me to call it The Muffin Manual, or Manifesto, or something like that, but I told him I didn't have time to be writing books. Not yet, anyway, but that I'd keep it in mind for when I retire."

"But you'll be staying on here, won't you?" asked one of the women. "Working for the new owner?"

"Oh no, I know a baby who needs taking care of," said Jessie, sitting back and crossing her arms. "I'm

going along with Cassie here and her momma to mind
Erin while *her* momma, Cindy, goes back to school."

I watched the way the sunlight hit the flowers in the
center of the table and just let my mind drift until my
mother came to the door, calling, "Time for the bride
and groom to cut the cake," and waving for us all to
move inside.

While everybody crowded to get into the dining
room, Megan and Billy and Tommy and I cut through
the kitchen and went in the other door, ending up
right next to Will and Emma. I noticed that my
grandmother had changed out of her church clothes
and back into a jeans skirt and a yellow T-shirt, that
Will had taken off his coat and tie and rolled up his
sleeves. They were regular people again. Only married.

"Speech, speech!" cried someone in back.

"Oh my, well, I don't think so," said Emma, shaking
her head and brushing a strand of hair out of her face.
"Unless you have something to say, William."

"Public speaking has never been my forte," said
Will, "so I'll make it brief. Thank you all mightily for
coming to share our happiness. Now let's eat cake."

"Hear, hear," said Billy's dad.

"Hear, hear," said everybody else.

We ate the cake, and the grownups had coffee, too.
Miss Betty played the piano, and when she got tired,

Will's son Frank played for a while, and when *he* got tired, Megan and I played "Heart and Soul" a bunch of times, till everybody yelled for us to stop. Guests wandered from room to room and out onto the porch and back again. People laughed, and the jabber of voices seemed to fill the air. Then, as if by some special signal, we all moved out back, and it was time for Emma and Will to leave.

All of a sudden, Emma seemed to have a lot to say— to Mom and Jessie, to Cindy and me—about how to take care of things at the Spindrift. "Clean sheets and towels every day. Check the books in the Ebb Tide before the new people come in on Saturday. We'll be in Williamsburg, and you have the number if there're any problems. Now let me—"

Will laughed and opened the car door. "I think it's time," he said.

Thirteen

MOST OF THE GUESTS went home after Will and Emma left, but those who didn't settled into the living room to talk while the caterer's helpers started to clean up. Megan, Tommy, Billy, and I went around front, dumped our shoes on the porch, and kept on going, to the beach.

"Oh, wow," said Billy. "This is wild. We don't have oceans in Santa Fe, and this is awesome." He and Tommy moved down to the water's edge, while Megan and I sat on the sand, turning to look back at the Spindrift. I stared at the house, trying to memorize every shingle, every shutter, every spindle in the porch railing. And I thought how maybe Emma was right when she said that it's what's in our head and heart that matters most.

"Are you packed yet?" asked Megan.

"Pretty much," I said. "We don't move till the first of October, but we can start taking the small stuff out this week."

"And what about your grandmother and Will—when they get back from Williamsburg, I mean?"

"They'll stay here till the Carsons settle for the Spindrift and for after that they have a condo at Sea Colony. With an extra bedroom for when I want to stay over."

Just then Billy's father called that it was time to go, and we all headed up from the beach, trailing past the side of the house to where the rest of them were waiting by the car. There were goodbyes all around, with promises that Mom and Cindy and Erin and I would maybe someday go to Santa Fe, that Billy and his mother and father would come back to Bethany.

"This whole place is awesome," Billy said out the window as the car pulled away and turned at the corner.

When I got back inside, the house was empty and weirdly quiet. "Now what?" said Mom, sitting down at the kitchen table and spinning the lazy Susan. "What's everybody going to do this afternoon?"

"There's an eighth-grade car wash over at school, and Tommy and Megan and I are supposed to be there to work," I said. "Remember, Mom? I told you."

"My dad's going to drive us, once we've changed our clothes," said Tommy.

"And my mom'll bring us back," said Megan.

"I'm taking Erin for a walk," said Cindy. "Want to come, Mom?"

"No, thanks," my mother said. "I think I'll curl up with a good book, and if I fall asleep, so be it. It's been a busy morning."

At school Megan and Tommy were given bucket duty, and I was sent to the end of the driveway with a giant CAR WASH sign to sort of swoop people into the parking lot. They came all afternoon, people I knew and people I didn't know: teachers from school, parents, strangers just driving by, and even the minister—but in regular clothes this time.

It was getting late when Mrs. Quattlemayer pulled in. By then my sign was in tatters, and I bunched it up and shoved it into the trash as I followed her to the washing place. She checked to see that her windows were rolled up and stopped to speak to Megan and Tommy before coming over to where I was standing.

"How are you, Cassie? I haven't gotten a chance to see you outside of class since school started. Did you have a good summer?"

"Well," I said, stepping out of the way of the hose that Terry Waddell was swinging around, "a lot went on. Some good, some not so good. I mean, my sister had a baby, and now I have a niece named Erin. But she, Cindy, my sister, is getting a divorce and that means Mickey's gone—out of our lives, anyway. Except that he's still Erin's father. My grandmother Emma sold the Spindrift, and my mother bought a house. And just this morning Emma married Will. So now I have a grandfather."

"That *is* a lot for one summer," Mrs. Quattlemayer said, shaking her head. "Did you get it all down in your journal?"

"Some. A little," I said. "But things just kept happening."

"Store it up, Cassie. Store it up and sort it out. And maybe someday you'll write about it."

"Yeah, maybe," I said, standing back and watching as Tommy sloshed soapy water over Mrs. Quattlemayer's dented blue Honda. Watching and sort of smiling as the water from Megan's hose washed down over the car. "Maybe I will," I said.